DAVID PARK has written eight books including *The Big Snow*, *Swallowing the Sun*, *The Truth Commissioner*, *The Light of Amsterdam* and, most recently, *The Poets' Wives*. He has won the Authors' Club First Novel Award, the Bass Ireland Arts Award for Literature, the Ewart-Biggs Memorial Prize, the American Ireland Fund Literary Award and the University of Ulster's McCrea Literary Award, three times. He has received a Major Individual Artist Award from the Arts Council of Northern Ireland and been shortlisted for the Irish Novel of the Year Award three times. He lives in County Down, Northern Ireland.

BY THE SAME AUTHOR

Oranges from Spain

The Healing

Stone Kingdoms

The Big Snow

Swallowing the Sun

The Truth Commissioner

The Light of Amsterdam

The Poets' Wives

The Rye Man

DAVID PARK

BLOOMSBURY

LONDON · NEW DELHI · NEW YORK · SYDNEY

First published in Great Britain by Jonathan Cape in 1994
This paperback published 2015

Bloomsbury Publishing Plc
50 Bedford Square
London
WC1B 3DP

www.bloomsbury.com

Bloomsbury is a trademark of Bloomsbury Publishing Plc

Bloomsbury Publishing, London, New Delhi, New York and Sydney

A CIP catalogue record for this book is available from the British Library

ISBN 978 1 4088 6602 3

10 9 8 7 6 5 4 3 2 1

Printed and bound in Great Britain by CPI Group (UK) Ltd, Croydon CR0 4YY

to Helen Jackson and Eileen Lindsay

THERE WAS STILL TIME to change his mind. All he had to do was knock off the indicator light and drive away. The line of oncoming cars preventing him making the right turn through the open gates and into the curved driveway, showed no sign of breaking. Behind, the road was still clear with no following car to be confused by a change of signal. He stared at the high, wrought-iron gates, their intricate design dating them to an older period, and the tall birch and elm trees which formed a screen behind the redbrick wall, obscuring any view of the building. All he had to do was knock off the indicator and drive on past – that's all he had to do. Its noise grew louder, blocking out the sound of the radio, steady and precise like the rising beat of his heart. He stared at the faces of the passing drivers, but it felt as if he was invisible to them and no one returned his glance, or turned their eyes towards him. And then suddenly the road was clear, the noise of the indicator greater than his senses could bear, and he was driving through the open gates.

The driveway was bordered on both sides by thick wedges of shrubbery and overhanging trees whose skinny black branches darkened it with shadows, the only colour where their last shot leaves shivered in the wind. As he drove underneath, one fluttered on to the windscreen and lay trembling like a veined and yellowed moth. A car went by with a nurse driving, one hand pushing her thick black hair into shape, as if she had just taken off her cap. Round the first bend he had a view of the house – old, imposing, probably Victorian, wearing a beard of ivy which had been clipped back sharply from upper windows. A red splurge of Virginia creeper fanned across a wide wall and neat box hedging edged the gravel driveway leading to the front doors. The white window frames looked new but only the television aerials seemed incongruously modern. It felt like driving into the past, a journey that no longer brought its old reassurance, because he knew now that even the past could change and was fixed only in the faltering and flawed frame of memory.

He touched his brakes as a man in blue overalls pushed a wheelbarrow across the drive. The man nodded and smiled a gap-toothed greeting as he crossed in front of the car, and for the first time his secret conviction that he would be able to recognise the man he had come to visit struck him as arrogant and inconceivably foolish. Twenty-seven years had passed, and while the image he carried in his head from that moment in boyhood would remain with him for ever, he forced himself to admit that it could hardly be expected to bear any relation to the present. He looked again at the man pushing the wheelbarrow. He was about the right age but apart from that he could see nothing which might link him with the object of his visit. He couldn't even tell if he was a gardener employed by the hospital or a patient and his uncertainty increased his growing feelings of doubt about what he was doing.

As he parked the car he tried to regain some of his old self-confidence which helped him take charge of things, and as he walked towards the front entrance he strode out with sure and deliberate steps, but the very consciousness of his actions told him that he had lost what had been instinctive. An elderly couple, hand in hand with a girl he assumed to be their daughter, moved slowly towards him, patiently guiding her hesitant and crooked steps. They smiled at him as he stood aside to let them pass and the girl said hello in a loud childish voice, her head lolling to one side. He returned her greeting in the friendly, interested tone he reserved for children, the words rising towards the recipient, but when they had passed he glanced furtively over his shoulder as they made their way along the path, and he was afraid. It was something he had come to recognise – the taste in his mouth, the loosening and then tightening of his stomach.

He looked up at the ivy-framed windows and was suddenly aware of faces watching him. The light on the glass robbed them of their features and bleached them pale and unshapen. One of the windows was half open and a curtain shifted gently in the breeze. The inside of the building added to his confusion. He hadn't known what to expect but the unspoken word 'institution' spawned a range of distorted images, many of them, he knew, outdated and originating in old films, but he had been unable to replace them with anything more corporeal until this moment. What struck him first was that, despite it conforming to his preformed stereotype in terms of its age, it had an open and spacious feel about it. Even the foyer he now found himself standing in had a light, informal air, and people – he assumed they were patients – seemed able to walk about where they willed. Sometimes they were assisted by a nurse or orderly and in the distance he could see someone being pushed in a wheelchair. Waiting at the sliding glass window marked 'Reception' he felt like a small boy in his own school, unsure whether to knock or wait until someone noticed his presence. A girl with Down's Syndrome carrying a neat pile of ironed laundry stopped when she saw him and rolled her eyes in exasperation.

'Has no one come out to you? They're desperate in that office.'

He shifted uneasily, unsure of what to say, but she didn't wait for any response, simply opened the office door roughly

3

and shouted that there was someone waiting. He watched her march off down the corridor with the air of someone very much in charge. When the glass slid open and a receptionist appeared they both smiled a kind of apology before he told her his name and the reason for his visit. She searched in a book on her desk and then phoned to inform someone of his arrival.

'Sister will be with you in a minute, if you'd just like to wait.'

He nodded and tried to make himself less conspicuous as he looked about. It felt strange to be on the outside of something looking in and he tried to blend into the background, unobserved, as he sought to gauge the nature of the place. Everywhere was clean and polished and although the distinctive smell of communal cooking drifted from somewhere, there were few of the characteristics of a hospital. There was a lot of wood panelling around, and the building had been modernised in a way that preserved some of the original features. He could hear a piano playing on some higher level and an occasional burst of ragged hand-clapping, strangely unsynchronised and staccato. But apart from the building itself, it didn't feel a million miles away from some sort of school, and as he told himself that it encouraged him as he prepared for the arrival of the Sister. He assumed it would be the one he had spoken to on the phone. He remembered that her tone had been neutral, even suspicious, and wondered how he should handle her. He had told her his real name and the person he wanted to see, and although she had stopped just short of asking him the reason for his proposed visit, he had constructed a vaguely credible response, throwing in a couple of times the fact that he was a primary school headmaster – something he found himself doing increasingly in situations where bona fide credentials were required. People

4

trusted headmasters and, in the country at least, like doctor or bank manager, it was one of the few remaining titles still able to engender a modicum of respect.

He would shake her hand, call her Sister a few times to convey a respectful acknowledgement of her status, dredge up a sprinkling of charm and she would be all right. He watched a girl approaching down the wide staircase, her hand trailing lightly along the bannisters the way a child is comforted by the continuity and solidity of touch. She was about thirty and almost pretty, with fair hair swept back from her face and held in place with a brightly patterned hairband that was out of sync with her age. When she reached the bottom of the stairs she smiled at him, a naïve coquettish smile that he sometimes saw on the faces of children. He thought she was going to speak but as her head jerked back in an action he recognised, he raised his arm protectively in time to stop her full-throated spit splattering against his face.

'I'm sorry about that. Sandra's having a bad day.'

The Sister handed him a tissue to clean his jacket, then walked off down the corridor after the girl. When she caught up with her, she put her arm round the girl's shoulders in a gesture of both sympathy and control, then guided her into a room out of sight. It was a few minutes before she returned and the small damp spots on his jacket were the only evidence of what had happened. He followed her up the stairs, aware that her posture and pace discouraged small talk and told him that she had other duties she considered more important than this to fulfil. As they walked he was suddenly conscious that he'd come empty-handed. But what did you bring twenty-seven years too late to someone who might not know who you were or be able to understand? He wanted the Sister to speak to him, to give him her approval, advice on how he should handle the visit, but she seemed deep inside her own world, indifferent to his needs. As she led the way she paused from time to time to close a door or glance into a room. He had to say something; he didn't want it to be like this. From somewhere down the corridor the hand-clapping reached a broken crescendo then slowly faded into a solitary, insistent beat, over and over until it, too, vanished into its own silence.

THEY STOOD IN THEIR ROWS with curious upturned faces like so many stooks of corn. A few did elaborate stage whispers behind screening hands, some were smiling without realising it, while others shuffled and fidgeted in anticipation. Someone hacked out a rasping cough and immediately it was echoed by a sympathetic chorus. The youngest children stood close to the stage, some of them holding hands with their neighbours, the oldest ranged along the back of the hall, the occasional head of a tall child sticking up like a sunflower, all of them staring up at him with expectant faces. Even their teachers who stood stiffly at the sides like warders stared intently, keen to evaluate his first public performance. It felt too rigid, too impersonal.

He had a crazy impulse to do something outrageous – an Elvis Presley impersonation, swing like Tarzan on one of the climbing ropes which lay tethered lifelessly at the side of the hall. It was an impulse which often came when faced with an audience, born out of nervousness but also the knowledge that a performance was required. He re-shuffled the cards inside his head until he had them matched and sequenced.

'Good morning. Welcome back to the first day of a new school year. I hope you all had a good summer. It won't surprise you, I'm sure, to hear that I've a few things to say, but I think you'd probably be a bit more comfortable if you all sat down.' He motioned with a slow drop of his hand, the rows collapsing instantly as if they had been sliced by the swing

7

of a scythe. Only the teachers remained standing, shifting a little in a self-conscious realisation of their conspicuous stance.

'First days are a time for introductions. Most of you won't know who I am, so I'll start by telling you my name. I'm called John Cameron – not too hard to remember – although when I was the same age as some of you younger ones, I used to have trouble spelling it, but I'm sure you're all too clever to have that problem. Before too long I hope to get to know each one of you, but you'll have to be patient with me until I learn your names.

'Today, I'm the new boy in school and it feels a little strange, but in some ways I'm not really a new boy at all, because quite a long time ago, on a bright September morning just like this, my mother brought me through the same school gates you came through and delivered me into the hands of a very strict lady called Miss Winters, the infant class teacher. Of course the school wasn't exactly the same then as it is now – it was much smaller for a start – but some things aren't too different. That day was the beginning of a happy time and I'm sure that with your help and co-operation, today is also going to be the beginning of another happy time in my life.'

He spoke for a few more minutes. They were still listening; he wouldn't risk losing them.

'The final thing that I'd like to say this morning is to tell you about the type of school which I'd like to be headmaster of. It's a school where people show care and consideration for each other, where people work hard and make the most of all the talents they have been given, and above all, a school where people are happy. Now, without too much noise, I'd like you all to stand up and we'll sing our hymn, "Morning Has Broken". I'm told you know the words but just in case anyone has forgotten, the overhead projector will put them up on the screen.'

He took a step back and nodded to Mrs Haslett at the piano, who immediately dropped her raised hands like the talons of some bird of prey swooping on its victim, and set up a loud introductory jangle of sound. He tried not to smile as the elaborate peck of her head signalled the moment for the children to join in. Their voices rang out clear and high as they sang with childish sincerity. Early morning sunlight slipped between the lattices created by the wall bars and washed over the raised faces. It felt good. He had made the right decision. He wished Emma were there to see it, to listen to the singing voices, and then surely any of her lingering doubts would vanish. Headmaster of his old primary school, for some perhaps not the pinnacle of an educational career, but not something to be sneered at. It had a warm feeling of neatness about it, like a compass completing a circle.

He had inherited a school of just over two hundred pupils, seven teaching staff, a secretary and Eric the caretaker. Unlike some rural schools where falling rolls threatened, their future numbers were healthy. The traditional bedrock of farming stock continued to be prolific in their procreation, often siring into mature years, producing what was described as 'a wee late one', and the past decade had seen the growth of numerous housing developments often with words like Grange or Dale in their titles, and where all the streets were named after trees, the developers eschewing traditional townland names in favour of nomenclature designed to appeal to the young middle class. There was also an influx of Belfast commuters who bought up sites for ever-growing sums of money and built bungalows on them. Some of the roads he had known as a child had been developed out of recognition in this piecemeal way to the very limits of their capacity. It had prompted a cynical new definition of rotation – barley, maize, bungalow. A few took their children to Belfast prep schools, but most

9

made the decision to send them to their local schools, some perhaps seeing it as a means of assimilation, others as a guarantee of a solidly traditional education where children learned tables and spellings and didn't grow up looking down their noses at people who didn't go touring France for their holidays. It was this group of newcomers who ensured the growth of the school.

Now, as he sat in his office, he felt first a crazed recklessness – they had actually entrusted the keys of the kingdom to him – and he stared at the closed door. Outside he could hear footsteps scampering to classrooms like mice in a roofspace. Occasionally, laughter, a name called, the slower, heavier tread of an adult. In a few minutes an almost silence settled, broken only by the sound of a closing door or the high-pitched bleep of the office word processor. A sudden pang of loneliness stung him as if he had been peremptorily and irredeemably cut off from the life all around him. There was, too, a feeling of redundancy, an uncertainty as to his function or purpose. What did a headmaster actually do all day? Those headmasters he knew guarded the secret as if it were the most sacred of Masonic mysteries.

He made a start by opening the mail. There was already a stacked pile which had accumulated over the summer months. Three circulars from the Area Education Board about the purchase of heating oil, new regulations relating to the employment of cleaning staff and changes in superannuation payment, a letter from the local Girl Guides requesting the use of the school hall for their winter display evening. A letter from a Mrs Roulston saying that owing to her husband's employment circumstances she would be taking her son on holiday during term-time and apologising for any inconvenience caused. Another letter from the Board about purchasing procedure, a road safety competition and assorted catalogues from publishing companies. Not the most exciting start to his first day, but he drafted replies to the two letters which required them, and when he had finished, started to think about making the office look the way he wanted, personalising it, removing what remained of his predecessor.

Edwin Reynolds had taken early retirement and had known he was leaving for some time, but the small room looked as if he had simply dropped his burden and decamped. The calendar still displayed the thirtieth of June as if a date too sweet to give up to transience, and his desk contained a miscellany of small personal items. As well as the usual and expected things like pens and paper clips there was an Acme Thunderer whistle, a Swiss penknife, a box of teabags and a confiscated criminalia of catapults, dried-up conkers and stink bombs. He turned the drawers upside down over the bin the caretaker had supplied. It felt like he was clearing out the temple, making a clean start. Reynolds would not be back, happy to have made his home run and at that very moment was probably lifting his golf clubs into the boot of his car or dead-heading the roses. He had been Principal for over twenty years and was probably only too glad to find a bolthole as the waves of change began to break about his head. It was a common pattern, as a generation of men accustomed to being potentates, and in some cases despots, who had merely to ensure that the wheels turned smoothly, suddenly found themselves the supposed pivot of educational change with a shower of initiatives falling about their heads like confetti at a wedding. The installation of the computer terminal in his office had probably been the last straw.

The limitations of his educational perspectives and his personality were reflected in the office he had sat in for those twenty years without having felt the need to imbue it with the slightest manifestation of individuality. A sterile, functional little box, probably unchanged in all that time apart from the recent additions of carpet, a year planner, and overlaid pages of yellowing paper – phone numbers of substitute teachers, Health and Safety Regulations – looking like the peeling skins of some putrefying onion. In the two filing cabinets were only empty manilla folders and copies of school reports.

The telephone rang as he had just finished clearing away the final remnants from his predecessor's desk. It made him start a little, then smile. It was his secretary telling him his wife was on the line.

'Well, how's it going? You haven't done anything stupid yet?'

'No, just an Elvis Presley impersonation in assembly. It went down well. It's nice of you to ring. What're you doing now?'

'I've just had a shower – it leaks – and after breakfast I'm going to get on with clearing those outhouses. What're you doing?'

'Exorcising the ghost of Reynolds.' He dropped his voice to a whisper. 'Listen to this Emma, when I opened the drawers of his desk they were full of girlie magazines!'

'You're joking, John.'

He lingered over the shock in her voice for a few seconds, then couldn't hold it any longer, and as she realised she had been wound up her laughter joined with his.

'I must be still asleep to have fallen for that one!'

They chatted for a few minutes about their respective plans for the day and then she wished him good luck and was gone. He wished there had been more time to talk.

As he put the phone down he tried to hold on to the sound of her laughter. He had not heard a lot of it recently. Maybe the move to the country and a new house would be good for her, help her to heal more quickly. She seemed to be gradually shedding some of her strongest doubts, and getting the house into some sort of shape required most of her energy and thought. Perhaps too, if she was able to turn one of the outhouses into a studio she would be able to take up her work again and ease herself out of the depression her loss had brought. It was strange the way he always thought of it as her loss when he shared it too. Maybe he coped with it better, maybe though he didn't always believe it, his loss hadn't been as great as hers. He didn't know.

He started to unpack the items he had brought in a cardboard box, and to find a place for each of them. On his desk he placed the framed photograph of his last P7 class – he was standing with them at the top of the dry ski slope and after the photograph had been taken they had pushed him off, cheering his shaky journey to the bottom. On top of the filing cabinet he displayed the farewell card the children had made in Art and signed by every child in the school, then lifted out an unframed black and white photograph. It was his own primary class, taken in the school playground against the wall of the building, back row sentry straight, front row knees locked, arms folded. He called a silent roll of the names, only a couple eluding him, and paused over his own image. A buoyant, optimistic face with restless inquisitive eyes, wearing a stippled mask of freckles. Eyes which always wanted to know the secret of everything. Tall, even then.

He held the photograph gently, carefully; the past was something that was important to him. He looked at his whitened plimsolls. After the heaviness of winter shoes it used to feel like his feet had grown wings, making him want to run for no purpose other than the pleasure of his own speed. He brought the picture closer. The soles looked wafer thin and he smiled at the thought of the cushioned, thick-soled trainers that children now wore to school, as much to ensure their street cred as to engage in any physical activity, tongues and latticed laces shooting halfway up their shins.

There were more objects to be unpacked. The spoof front-page story with the headline, 'Cameron KO's Mike Tyson in First Round', a couple of Emma's small water-colours, one of his cricket trophies, and his 'world's greatest teacher' mug. While he was in the process of arranging everything there was a knock on the door, but despite his invitation no one entered.

It was a child – a girl with brown eyes, a ponytail decorated with brightly coloured butterfly bobs, and a hand that plucked at the hem of her shirt as she let her rehearsed message fly free like a small bird out of a cage.

'Miss McCreavey says P5 have no jotters.'

He cupped his head in his hands and opened his mouth and eyes wide in mock horror. 'No jotters! My goodness, what are we going to do?'

He brought her in and sat her down like the first visitor to a new house. She sat on her hands nervously, her eyes taking in as much of the room as she could do discreetly.

'What's your name?'

'Kerry Clark.'

'Kerry. And would you be related to the Bob Clark who has the shoe shop in Market Street?'

She nodded her head.

'I used to play cricket with your father. Do you think if I come down to his shop some Saturday he'd sell me a pair of those trainers you pump up like you do a bicycle tyre?'

She nodded again and smiled for the first time.

'Now, Kerry, I think we'd better see what we can do about those jotters. Can't have P5 sitting with nothing to write on. Come down to the office and we'll see if we can't find some.' He led her the short distance to the secretary's office and held open the door for her to enter.

'Mrs Patterson, we have a terrible problem. Kerry has just come to tell me that P5 have no jotters.'

Mrs Patterson didn't return his smile but bristled as if some slight had been inherent in his words. 'Mr Cameron, I've checked the requisitions and Miss McCreavey didn't order any jotters.' She held out a copy for his inspection but he looked past it into her face with confusion as she continued. 'It's here in black and white. Exercise books, A4 paper, manilla paper, sugar paper, tracing paper, Pritt sticks. No jotters.' She stepped back behind her desk with the air of someone who had just presented her argument to the jury, appealed to their sense of justice and now awaited the verdict with a deep conviction of the righteousness of her case.

'I'm sure you're right, Mrs Patterson, but can we not give P5 a set of jotters? Do we not have plenty in the stationery store?' He stared deliberately past her, almost in slow motion, into the narrow little store.

'We do have jotters but they're ones the other class teachers have ordered and if I give them out some other class will end up going short.'

'I'll tell you what we'll do then. You give Kerry a set of jotters and I'll order some more. Would that solve our problem?'

But she wasn't easily appeased. 'Stationery requisitions take a long time to come through. What if someone runs out before they arrive? I'll end up getting the blame.'

He was a patient man. He could keep it up much longer than she could sustain her resistance and he made sure his voice contained no trace of irritation. 'If that happens they can use exercise books or A4 paper.'

He stayed to watch her count out the jotters, her reluctance apparent in each movement, as if she was doling out her life savings. As he opened the door for the child to leave he called after her. 'Tell P5 to make sure they use up every line. We don't want any waste. Paper doesn't grow on trees!'

When he turned back to the office Mrs Patterson was busying herself in paperwork, seemingly oblivious to his presence, but when she spoke the edge had gone out of her voice and she seemed intent on explaining. 'Mr Reynolds always insisted that each teacher be responsible for their own stationery. He was very strict about it.'

He smiled and nodded as if to show he understood and that she was absolved from any personal blame. When she handed him a clutch of forms which needed his signature he signed them with only a perfunctory glance at their contents. He didn't want to get off on the wrong foot with her. He was well aware that an efficient secretary could run a school single-handed and deflect much of the brain-curdling paperwork which flooded in every day. She, too, was now conciliatory in tone.

'At break-time I always took Mr Reynolds a cup of tea and a biscuit. Would you like me to do that?'

'That's very kind of you, Joan, but I thought I'd probably take my break in the staffroom each morning. Maybe some mornings, though. Thanks very much.'

She had been Reynolds' secretary for ten years. It would take them a while to get to know each other. By reputation she was efficient, reliable and didn't appear to have had any problem adapting to the word processor, or any of the other technology which had recently arrived. She was in her late forties, dressed a little austerely, but he was confident he could win her over.

'And how do you like working here Joan? Not many quiet moments, I suppose?'

'Busy all day, Mr Cameron. It never stops. Apart from the admin and the phone, it's like a shop. Children looking for plasters for scratched knees, dinner tickets, sorting out lost property. Never a dull moment.'

'Sure isn't it keeping you young looking. Maybe later on in the week we'll have a chat about your job and any ideas you have about it. In the meantime I'd be grateful if you could keep on doing the excellent job you've been doing for the school, and if there's anything you want me to look after, give me a shout.'

She thanked him and started to edit a file on the processor. The green light of the screen filled with white lines of type. As he went out he could hear the soft click of her fingers on the keys.

*

Until break-time he dealt with a couple more phone calls – a student teacher asking if she could do her observation with them, a mother enquiring about music tuition – signed more forms, and finished the rest of his unpacking. He could still feel the presence of Reynolds in the room, but he knew it would fade as the days passed, and as he cleared the last assorted debris of his predecessor the bell rang for break.

Within a few seconds everywhere was alive with the rush of feet and childish voices. His office was beside the staffroom and soon he could hear the sound of the arriving teachers' voices, the water heater being switched on and cups being taken from cupboards. He had decided he wouldn't join them on this first morning, not intrude on their desire to discuss him and their estimation of the prospects for the coming year, and instead he put on his jacket and went into the corridor. Eric was ushering the final stragglers into the playground.

Outside the air felt clean and fresh after the dusty confines of the office. Strong bright sunlight gave everywhere a lingering feel of summer and the shouts and squeals of the children sliced through the air like the wings of birds. He set off on a leisurely circuit of the building, pausing now and again to simply look around him. The front of the school was largely unchanged since that day he had first entered as a pupil, but as over the years numbers had grown, the school had been extended in a piecemeal manner. Three additional classrooms had evolved from the original two-roomed building, followed more recently by the addition of an assembly hall, two further classrooms, office facilities and two mobile classrooms. While it was not perhaps the best planned school building he had seen, it wasn't the worst and it had a solid homely character which he liked. It also had the benefit of an attractive open setting which city schools rarely had. At the rear, beyond the playgrounds, was a grass area which swept to a hawthorn hedge. Beyond that stretched open fields, hedgerows and on a clear day, the Mourne mountains.

It was on this grass area that most of the children were playing, the patterns of their movements changing constantly like light on water. Bright little knots glistened then unwound outwards into flight, while others pulled tight in huddled, animated discussions. Some boys pushed each other in pretend roughness while others played football with a tennis ball. As he walked through them, children careered across his path. He almost collided with a boy wearing a Bart Simpson T-shirt proclaiming, 'I didn't do it, you didn't see me do it, you can't prove anything.' A very small boy offered him a drink from his plastic water bottle and he patted him on the head in reply. Pairs of children sat on the grass playing their Nintendo Game Boys and a tiny circle of girls played some sort of card game. There was a familiarity about their play which reassured him as they flowed about him, some so engrossed in their play that they did not notice his presence, and he felt happy.

He paused to listen to the lilting chant of a cluster of skipping girls, and the syncopated swish and slap of the rope on the playground:

'On the hillside stands a lady
Who she is I do not know
All she wants is gold and silver
All she wants is a nice young man.'

The rope slapped louder and faster, turning with the cadence of laughter as the skippers eluded its twists.

Gold and silver in their laughter – he didn't want any of it to end but he knew it was almost time. The tennis ball landed at his feet and he kicked it back. The sunlight was warm on his face, he didn't want to go back to Reynolds' office. It was the same hawthorn hedge which had bound his childhood play, the squat, spiky barrier into which they had pushed each other and then returned to class with a red tracery of scratches and occasionally a black-headed thorn prick, which the teacher had worked out with a needle sterilised in boiling water, while they stared down the great corsetted valley of her bosom.

There was a small girl sitting crouched at its base down at the farthest corner, almost part of it. Only the blonde colour of her hair made her perceptible. She squatted still and small and he looked for the other players of the game from whom she was hiding but could see none. Perhaps she had hidden too well. And then the bell rang and the flowing, divergent pattern of play coalesced and flooded back towards the school. When he looked back to the hedge, the girl had gone.

*

The foyer depressed him. It wasn't a big space but it was the area which created the first impression of the school. The navy paint on the walls darkened it, and from ground to child shoulder height, it was pitted with tiny white indentations where the plaster's daily contact with schoolbags and lunch boxes had left it looking like a satellite picture of the moon's surface. There was a long black stripe where something had been trailed along it and apart from a sign which instructed all visitors to report to the office, the only objects decorating the walls were an ancient framed school saving certificate and a dog-eared Green Cross Code poster. With a little imagination it could be turned into a focal point for the school, somewhere which presented a better impression of its life and work. Somewhere which signalled the type of environment he intended to create. He wanted everything to be different, to look different − everywhere to carry his signature. But he had little time to give it further thought.

On the way back to his office he met some of the staff returning to their rooms and he smiled and nodded at them. Part of him envied the rest of their morning and he would have swopped with anyone who might have offered. His job still felt strange, like wearing a new suit you were not quite sure fitted properly, and had not really decided whether you liked it or not. He held a door open for a child carrying a tape recorder, encouraged another to tie his shoelace. Little wisps of grass could be seen on the tiled corridor where they had stuck in the grooves of trainers, then dropped out.

It was time to meet the troops. It had been his intention to visit some of the classrooms briefly, show his face, start off that relationship of encouragement and support which he hoped would be one of his main characteristics. Now the moment had arrived, he felt a little nervous, unsure of where to start or how to carry it off. It was important his arrival did not carry any heavy overtones, or appear like some kind of early inspection.

He studied the timetable on the notice-board to the side of his desk and looked at the names of his staff. He had already formed impressions of them from the Baker day and the discreet enquiries he had made. There were obvious pluses and minuses, and in some cases he hoped his first impressions had been wrong. A school staff was not like managing a football club. There were no free transfers or big name signings to bolster up a struggling team. You were stuck with what you inherited.

He tried to be positive, optimistic about the people with whom he was about to work. Perhaps for the reason that he had already taken a liking to Fiona Craig, he decided to start with her infant class. The door, decorated with butterfly transfers, was partly open, but he knocked before he entered. She was engrossed with a group of children playing in water and did not notice his entry until her classroom assistant pointed him out. She dried her hands on her apron as she approached, and he was pleased to see that she was smiling. The whole room was awash with colour – reds, yellows, blues – with stencilled numbers, letters of the alphabet, clowns' faces, posters of animals and cartoon characters. There seemed to be children everywhere, sitting and drawing at the scaled-down tables, playing in sand with buckets and spades, hammering pegs into blocks with wooden mallets, dressing up in costumes. Most were too busy to notice his entrance. A few looked up at him with curiosity.

'Just called in Mrs Craig, to see how things were going. Everybody seems to be having a good time. I wouldn't mind having a go myself at some of these things.'

'Well,' she laughed, 'I think you're probably a bit too tall for the Wendy house, but you could join in the Mad Hatter's tea party if you like. Sarah, pour Mr Cameron a nice cup of tea.'

With her tongue peeping out of the corner of her mouth the child carefully lifted the yellow plastic teapot and poured a cupful of blue water. He bent down and, lifting it up, pretended to sip it.

'A very nice cup of tea, Sarah. Just what I really needed.'

Other children offered him cups. A small boy came and handed him his hammer for inspection. Soon he began to feel like a distraction, an interloper into their play, and already he could see Mrs Craig's gaze sweeping the room, anxious to see where her presence was needed. Two children had started to squabble over a spade in the corner of the sand area, so he complimented her on the attractiveness of the room and sought to excuse himself.

'I'll not get in your way any longer, Mrs Craig, it looks like world war three's about to break out in the sand pit. Good luck to you.'

As he was about to leave she called after him. 'Mr Cameron, there was talk at the end of last year of my classroom assistant having her hours cut, and I'd like to think there's been a change of mind. I can't see how I'd be expected to function here on my own.'

He tried to assure her that he'd no knowledge of it and it seemed an unlikely and undesirable possibility, but she seemed unconvinced.

'And, Mr Cameron, as you can see it's very cramped in here, we really need some sort of cloakroom space for the children to leave their outdoor coats and shoes. At the very least, pegs or a portable hanger. Oh, and Mr Reynolds promised me that he'd see that the leak in the roof was fixed. I had rain coming in like Niagara Falls all last winter and it doesn't create a very good impression for parents to see water dripping into a bucket.'

He stopped himself making a joke about water play and instead promised her that he would see it was fixed as soon as possible. The two children were now having an all-out tug-of-war over the spade.

'Oh, Mr Cameron.'

He turned again. She seemed determined to have her money's worth.

'Good luck!'

He thanked her and smiled. Over her shoulder he could see the victor of the tug-of-war using the spade to smack his adversary. When he closed the door the butterflies seemed to hold a vibrant delicacy, almost as if at any second they might fly away.

A few yards further down the corridor he called on Laura Fulton, the probationary teacher. He paused outside the door for a few seconds, listening to her voice, and when he entered she made a movement that was alarmingly close to a curtsey and then coloured with embarrassment. It was the first day of her first teaching job and when he looked at her he was unsettled momentarily by how young she looked – a slip of a girl with brown eyes and thick black wiry hair pulled into a ponytail, standing in front of a room full of children. She wore a red top with black silhouettes jogging across it and matching red cords, and she looked so fresh that he smiled longer than he meant to. Behind her the class stared at him, wide-eyed, and the children grouped round circular tables who had their backs to him swivelled on their chairs.

'Well, Laura, how's it been going? Ready to jack it in yet? They say the first ten years are the worst.'

She laughed and lightly flicked her ponytail out of her collar.

'It's going quite well. I've been reading to them and they've been very good. It'll be easier when I learn all their names.'

He was glad he had a probationary teacher. If she possessed any aptitude at all for the job he would help her become a good teacher, help her understand what it was all about and in return he would gain her loyalty. It was a pity she would never realise that he had saved her from Reynolds. The children had started to talk, some chairs scraped and she was glancing anxiously at the class, worried that the rising current of noise was a reflection on her control. Turning her head sideways she gave them a loud shush.

'Noise isn't such a terrible thing. It just means they're still alive.' He told her his joke about the cross-eyed teacher who couldn't control his pupils and then she asked if she was to show him her lesson plans each week.

'I sincerely hope not. I'll look at them if you want, but I'm happy for you to get on with the job and we'll talk at regular intervals about how things are going. I see, too, there's a probationers' induction course during the year, but a fat lot of use it'll do you, and I know because I've taken two of them. They always end up as a bitching session where everyone swops their horror stories, compares the size of their classes and number of free periods, then either goes away feeling hard done by or counting themselves lucky. But nobody really learns anything.'

She was looking up at him, her brown eyes and unbroken attention encouraging him to flow on.

'The classroom's the only place you can learn. In teaching there's lots of ways that are wrong but there's no one right way, so be confident, step out, don't be frightened to make mistakes and learn from them. That's what it's all about.'

She thanked him and the genuineness of her tone made him feel good. Two small girls came up hand in hand and one of them said that her friend needed to go to the toilet. He held the door open for them and took his leave, watching the children's diffident progress down the corridor, unused to being out on their own.

Mrs Patterson appeared. There was a phone call for him in the office – a sales rep trying to sell him a new reading scheme which was supplemented by a range of computer software. He listened politely for a while and then declined the package as being outside the range of his budget. There was a parent waiting to collect her daughter who had been sick and he offered sympathy and made some comment about first day nerves. There were more returns and an inventory of furniture to be completed. When he resumed his tour Miss McCreavey's class were in the middle of a music lesson and the air vibrated with the tinkle of chimes and finger cymbals. Some pupils played recorders, and through the glass in the door he could see Miss McCreavey beating time on a yellow-skinned tambourine, but whatever tune it was seemed to have got lost, and he passed on by.

As he walked it was the skipping song of the girls he heard again, the swish and slap of the rope, the laughter in their voices. He stored it safely in his memory. Ahead, light angled through a high window and splashed against the walls, illuminating the smear of small fingerprints. He paused for a second and touched the wall, pressing the tips of his own fingers into it. Perhaps if he could hold tightly to their song it might drown out the other sounds which had returned to seep through his dreams. But then the light faded and he was conscious again only of the recorders' high-pitched whine, the tinkle and thud of the tambourine.

There was a boy standing outside Mrs Haslett's room and it was obvious from his sheepish stance that he had been ejected. When the boy saw him coming, he leaned off the wall and tried to appear as if his presence there had some legitimate purpose.

'Are you waiting for a bus?' There was no reply. 'What's your name?'

'Mark.'

'I don't think there's a bus on this route, Mark.'

'I've been put out of class.'

'What for, Mark?'

The boy shuffled his feet and patted the wall behind him with the palms of his hands, then stared vacantly into space.

'I can ask Mrs Haslett if you like.'

'Calling Simon Porter names.'

'And what did you call Simon Porter?'

'Don't want to say, Sir.'

'Well then, it must've been something pretty bad.'

'He called me names first. He's always calling me names but he never gets into trouble.' Tears were beginning to well up in the boy's eyes and he was pushing himself back against the wall in a kind of rhythm.

'What did Simon Porter call you, Mark?'

'He said I had AIDS and he told the other boys not to go near me.'

'And do you have AIDS, Mark?'

'No.' A fat globular tear leaked down his cheek.

'And what did you call Simon Porter?'

'It's rude, Sir.'

'Whisper it to me . . . a bit louder. I can't hear you.'

'A willie watcher.'

'And is Simon Porter a willie watcher, Mark?'

'No, Sir.'

'Well, then, it all sounds a bit stupid to me and it's ended up in a bit of a mess, hasn't it?' He handed the boy his handkerchief. 'Go down to the boys' toilets and splash your face and when you feel OK come back up and we'll get you back into class.'

He nodded and handed back the crumpled handkerchief, then set off quickly down the corridor.

When he entered Muriel Haslett's room she was haranguing her class and she stopped in mid-flow and stared at him, her initial embarrassment changing to irritation at his interruption. For a second he thought she was going to ask him what he wanted, but she regained her composure and assumed the patronising tone he had come to associate with her.

Although he knew her already by reputation, in the short time they had worked together he had developed a dislike for her. Her contribution on the Baker day had been negligible and negative, and it was perfectly clear without words being used that she resented his arrival in the school. Perhaps she had envisaged herself as the new vice-principal in the event of Kenneth Vance, the internal candidate, proving successful. It was obvious that she was going to be difficult, a source of obstruction. He knew that she saw herself as the first lady of the school, enlisting some and intimidating others into her corner.

She was in her late forties, had slumped into overweight but wore expensive and stylish clothes. She had tightly-permed hair which was coloured a mauvish tint and blue-framed glasses with thick lenses that made her eyes round and owl-shaped. From their first introduction she had made it obvious that she would not be buying whatever it was he had to sell, adopting a kind of superior weariness, a spurious wisdom which suggested she had arrived at a state of excellence which needed neither modification nor appraisal. There was some-thing almost fascinating about her awfulness and he was intrigued to see her in front of children. They sat in rows at double desks in straight rows, silent but surreptitiously watching and listening, obviously conditioned in how to behave in front of a visitor because no one spoke, not even a furtive whisper behind hands. They were working on some exercise out of textbooks. From the patterns on the pages it looked like maths. In one corner was a nature table, furbished with the remains of last year's collection – dried up birds' nests, some jagged cacti, something that looked like a sheep's skull, assorted bones and a few wilted plants. On the back walls were three science posters, one of the corners flapping over where the drawing pin was missing, and faded pages of children's writing. Looking around, he felt like someone who had just purchased a property and found his first piece of damp rot.

She was talking down to him, jokingly berating her pupils' inability to master some new concept but he hardly heard what she was saying for thinking of what he was going to do with her. She was talking about his mother – she was the choir mistress of his mother's church – and it was the second time she had spoken about her. It was her way of saying, 'I know who you are and where you come from.' He made some polite reply then cut across her line of conversation with a question about the boy in the corridor. She flustered a little and mumbled something which made little sense and he pressed home his momentary advantage by diverting suddenly into another avenue of thought, then excused himself and started to leave. At the door he paused.

'Mrs Haslett, could you please send Simon Porter to my room.'

'Now?'

'Yes, please.' As he spoke, he smiled deliberately at her then was gone.

*

After the boy had left he remembered the two occasions he had been sent to the headmaster's office. The first was in the company of James McMaster and Harry Gordon for having broken a window with a catapult. Gordon had fired the deadly shot but he and McMaster had been fingered as accomplices. The memory made him smile, but it faded as he remembered the thin white welt of pain which quivered the fingertips of both hands, and when the letter had arrived home his mother had taken the wooden spoon to the soft parts of his legs. The second time had been at the height of his temporary fame to receive a commendation for his part in the story that was on everyone's lips. He even had his name read out in assembly and a photographer from the local paper had arrived one afternoon to take his picture. It had been taken against the side wall of the school and when it appeared the following week his mother had given off to him for not having the wit to brush his hair before it was taken.

A small town hero. He remembered the feeling very clearly, the handshakes from older men, the whispers in church, the free bag of clove rock Mr McFaul had given him in his shop. He had worn his pride like a little badge – been pointed out to the uninformed and generally made a fuss of. He had lived off it for maybe a year, trading on it, cashing it in when other funds were low, and even now he knew some of the older people in the community still identified him by reference to it. His mother had kept all the newspaper cuttings and pasted them into a child's scrapbook. The memory of it felt as if it had been regenerated by his coming back to his old school, perhaps the final commendation, the reward he had finally come to claim.

Not even the thought of Mrs Haslett could tarnish that feeling. She was strong and she was cunning but he knew he held both the past and present cleanly and surely in his hands, cupping them in a chalice of self-belief. And now no child who came within the realms of his world, entered the gates of his school, would ever suffer like that again. He was not a religious person, but he did believe he carried some appointed kind of responsibility to see such a thing belonged only in the crinkled, yellowing pages of a faded newspaper.

He glanced out of the window and caught the arcing black flight of a crow flapping across the sky. He shivered as another memory shuffled towards the door he tried to keep tightly locked: a child's voice calling to him, the pleading, sobbing, breaking out of the mired blur of his dreams. His hand sought the consolation of the wooden grain of his desk, plucked at the calming reality of the wash of printed paper.

*

The lunchtime bell rang in his head like an alarm, the darkness of his thoughts suddenly disturbed by the rising sounds of released children. He could not decide whether the morning had dragged or gone quickly as children's heads bobbed by his window and from next door came voices and locker doors opening. It had been his intention to join the staff but now he wasn't quite so sure. Perhaps he should let the dust of his arrival settle a little before he joined them, maybe they would feel he was imposing himself on them, intruding in what they might consider to be their domain. As he hesitated, there was a knock at his office door and before he had time to respond he was looking at George Crawford, the chairman of his Board of Governors.

'Checking up on me already, George?'

'Get away with you. I've better things to do with my time. Just you plough a straight furrow and you'll not be seeing me more than you have to. I only called in to see if the seat fits you all right.' He lumbered into the office and slumped into the chair, his size and weight making the journey seem arduous. He declined the offer of a cup of tea and dabbed the sides of his mouth with a clean white linen handkerchief.

He had known George Crawford since childhood and he was never fully able to shake off those childish impressions. He remembered him as the generous host who held barn dances for church funds. A big man in a cowboy shirt that billowed out of his waistband, calling the dances, slapping his broad thigh in time to the music. He had sat high up in the piled bales of hay with the other younger children and watched their parents move with unexpected grace and shocking abandon, as fiddlers played and papery-winged moths fluttered frantically around the trembling, hissing oil lamps; outside, the breathing, rustling night. Getting carried home on your father's shoulders with sleep nestling in your eyes and clutching the bar of chocolate George had given all the children.

Now, though, he was a central character in the community, someone who had started out farming a modest family holding and then begun to deal in farm machinery, gradually establishing a very lucrative business which operated across the whole province. With commercial success had come all the trappings of wealth – the big house outside the town, the expensive car, but none of them had seemed to change the essence of his character as a practical man who was dismissive of all forms of pretension and disdainful of deference.

'And how are the troops shaping up?'

'Well, I've been round some this morning. I haven't had time to call with Mr Vance yet.'

'You're not missing much there. If thon boy smiled he'd crack his face. His father was just the same. Ran a local amateur operatic society, and looked down his nose at anyone who didn't think he was the bee's knees. He once asked me who Hank Williams was!' He paused and ran his palm across the bottom of his folded chin as if checking that he had remembered to shave. 'Vance must think I'm senile if he thought i'd hand over this school to a streak of piss like him. If I'd had my way he wouldn't even have been made vice-principal.'

He felt a little shocked by the description of Vance, uncomfortable at having one of his staff described in that way. 'They say he gets a good rate of passes in the qualifying exam,' he said defensively.

'Aye, I suppose that's true enough and that's what parents want, no doubting that these days. But you know how he got the vice-principal's job? It was that snake-in-the-grass Houston. I'd been away in London the week before and he'd canvassed the whole committee. It was all sewn up before I knew what was happening. Of course, it's purely coincidental that the Reverend Houston's wife is the leading lady of the operatic.' He was shaking his head as if cursing his own duplicity in the affair. 'I'm telling you now, John, we need to watch Houston. He's a devious bugger and he's always stirring it. Half the time it's that bitch of a wife winds him up. But the next governor's meeting he tries anything we'll see him coming and together we'll work out how to deball him.'

Children's heads flailed past the window, arms windmilling.

'I think I'll take that cup of tea. I don't suppose old Reynolds left anything stronger?'

'Only thing Reynolds left behind was this pile of unopened mail. Every time I start to work through it, some more pours in.'

He went to the office and asked Mrs Patterson for two cups of tea. While he was there, Eric presented him with two boys who had ventured out of school grounds, another who had been climbing a drainpipe in an attempt to retrieve a ball from the roof. Mrs Douglas was administering first-aid to a girl who had fallen and he winced as he saw the red, skinned knees. When he returned Mrs Haslett was standing in the open doorway, a china cup and saucer in one hand, while the other hand casually rested at right angles against the frame. She was exchanging some slightly flirtatious banter with George. With a show of ceremony, she dropped her arm to let him enter, but lingered in conversation for a few more seconds before moving away.

'Now there's a grand woman to have working for you,' he said, raising the china cup to his lips, its delicate floral pattern incongruous in the massive hand.

'You think so?' Their eyes met briefly over the rims of the cups and then there was a second of silence as each considered what to say.

'So you're not over-taken with Muriel, then?'

'Early days, George.'

'I know she can get on her high horse sometimes, but isn't it better having someone with a bit of character about them than a dry stick like Vance?'

He made a neutral, uncommitted reply.

'Listen, John, you're the man in the driving seat. You make the decisions, run the school. That's what we appointed you for and I don't doubt for a moment that you're big enough to do that. So just you steer your own course and don't pay heed to back seat drivers, even when their name is Muriel Haslett.' He drained the last dregs from his cup and ran his handkerchief across his mouth. 'And what about Miss Fulton, is she going to make the grade? At the interview she looked more like a waif than a teacher. Can we rely on her?'

'I think she'll be OK. I'll keep an eye out for her, make sure she gets plenty of help.' He watched as he stuffed the handkerchief back into his trouser pocket and slowly stood up, sending creases running through his suit like cracks in plaster. He offered his hand across the desk.

'Well, I'll wish you all the best and let you get on with the job. And remember, I'm only a phone call away, so never hesitate.'

He thanked him and watched his heavy journey to the door. He hesitated, though, before leaving.

'Listen, John. When I was a young buck round the town I used to drive a secondhand Morris Oxford, the miles had been round the clock but she was a lovely thing – a better car than the expensive pile of junk I drive now. And, well . . . I did a bit of courting from time to time and a certain Muriel Chambers as she was then, was no stranger to that back seat. So the next time the same lady gives you a hard time, just think of those creaking springs and maybe she won't seem quite so formidable.'

*

He sat in the empty office, his visitor's weight still imprinted on the chair. Lunch was over and already he could hear the clatter of footsteps in the corridors as the children returned to their rooms. He went out and watched as they streamed past, their faces flushed with the exertions of play and hair disarrayed. As the final stragglers regained their rooms, he suddenly realised he hadn't had anything to eat, and he returned to his office to rummage in his briefcase for his lunch box. He carried it next-door to the empty staffroom and switched on the water heater, then sank into one of the faded armchairs.

There was a tiny square of folded paper nestling beside the sandwiches. It was a cartoon of him flying through the air, wearing a mortar-board and a gown. Under the gown he was wearing a Superman tunic. He remembered the fragments of her laughter on the phone and he tried to piece them together into some better picture of the future. He thought of her working in the outhouses, her mind occupied, concentrating only on creating a studio. It was what she needed too – a new start. If only she could embrace it, give herself fully to it, everything might come all right again. As he looked around him he envied her freedom to splash paint about, her freedom to pull down and re-arrange to her own desires.

The staffroom was not much different from every other one he had ever been in, with a handful of shabby armchairs and coffee tables marked with white rings, a table and chairs ostensibly for marking and some lockers personalised by Garfield posters or stickers which said tired, predictable things like, 'You don't have to be mad to work here but it helps'. There was an old banda machine covered in blue fingerprints and on the notice-board were layers of circulars, old cover notes, union news-sheets. They were piled on top of each other, overlapping and out of date. A marked-off column on the board bore the title 'Headmaster's notices'. There was nothing on it except a postcard from Paris. He unpinned it and read, 'Wishing you all a successful new term. E. S. Reynolds.' The confirmation of a home run, the final smug message from blighty. He replaced it and had his lunch, thinking about his last visitor.

He liked Crawford, felt he could work with him. Maybe he was not the greatest educationalist in the world, but he had a generous spirit and had always made his regard for his new headmaster very clear. After he had applied for the post, George had turned up one Saturday afternoon during the tea interval of a cricket match he was playing in and announced after five minutes' casual conversation that the job was his. Both the suddenness and the conviction of the statement had

35

taken him by surprise, and when he had cautioned with talk of other candidates and the unpredictability of committee decisions, he had been told emphatically, 'You're the right size for the job.'

The right size for the job. That was about it. Local boy made good. He had always maintained his links with his home town, played for the cricket team, was seen occasionally at local functions. His family enjoyed the respect of the community and his mother still played an active role in the church. The right background, the right religion, the right size for the job.

Vance, the inside man, should have been his strongest rival, but he guessed while chatting to him before the interviews started that he wasn't going to perform well. He was too nervous, too stiff, obviously unable to bend from his own self-perception to meet alternative expectations. Vance could have been a problem but in the short time he had worked with him he had detected no depth of resentment or personal enmity. If anything, there was almost an indifference to the situation, as if his failure merely confirmed his judgement on life. Perhaps he already knew George's opinion of him and had harboured no genuine expectations.

He finished his lunch and rinsed his cup. He looked at the other mugs sitting upside down on the draining board and hesitated before he set his down beside them. It looked conspicuous and he moved it to the rear of the tight little knot. Somewhere in the distance he could hear the jangling chords of the piano and he was aware once more of life flowing round about him and his detachment from it.

He found Vance standing at the front of his class with a stop-watch in his hand. It was like the beginning of some sort of a race and at his signal heads dropped in unison and hands flipped over the booklets on their desks. There was a thick silence settling on the room, holding it fast and still like ice frozen over water. Only the scratch of pencils, the occasional shuffle. No one paused to look at him and when he spoke to Vance his voice sounded loud and intrusive. It was explained that they were practising their first test under the same constraints of time they would encounter in the real tests which would determine whether they gained a place in grammar school. He looked across the rows of bowed heads to the displays of geometrical patterns on the back wall, the neat rows of reading books and stacked exercise books. It was an ordered room designed to follow a precisely organised pattern.

Vance stood in his neat jacket and tie, distant, almost remote. He was in his late thirties, with thin, fair hair and gold-rimmed glasses which gave his face an ascetic quality. Above the blackboard was a poster of Mozart and it was obvious that music played an important role in his life. It was also becoming obvious that he was a friend of Haslett's and that they could prove a difficult duo if they acted in unison. It was important that he was able to establish some sort of working relationship with the man. Perhaps the fact that he was going to be teaching history to his class would be a help.

They stood for a few moments, struggling for things to say, their voices low as in church. Looking round he understood how Vance approached this final year of primary school. The emphasis was on practice, mechanical repetition, training in recognising types of questions and applying the correct methodology. Competition with each other, the recording of scores, class orders. He was suddenly conscious of a stale afternoon smell which made him want to open all the windows, let some fresh air in. Looking down finally at the children, no eyes met his and he felt a momentary urge to say something, to make some sort of contact, but he was conscious of Vance standing close by his side and he knew it would be considered a disruption. As he turned towards the door he noticed a head angled unusually at the back of the room. It was the blonde-haired girl he had seen kneeling by the hedge. Her tongue lolled from the corner of her mouth like a pink bookmark poking out from pages. She was sitting on her own and the movements of her hand showed that she was doing something different from the other children. As Vance showed him out, he had time only to see that she was holding a thick purple crayon, and he gauged by the concentration on her face that she was colouring something in, struggling to stay inside the lines.

*

In his office there was a phone call awaiting him. It was Liam Hennessy, the Principal of Holy Cross, the local Catholic primary school. He was phoning to wish him all the best in his new post and although they had never met they were soon using each other's first names. There was, too, another purpose to the call.

'Tell me now, John, how do you fancy a bit of Education for Mutual Understanding? I could never get that boy Reynolds interested, but what do you say?'

'Well, I'm all for mutual understanding. What had you in mind?'

'I don't right know yet . . .' He broke off to bark at some deviant nearby, '. . . but by all accounts the Department'll pour any amount of money down our throats if they think we're crossing the fence.'

He smiled, reassured that he was being invited to participate in the reality of a financial enterprise rather than some altruistic scheme. They agreed to get in touch and talk it over.

He opened more of the pile of post. A circular about school trips, a memo about United Nations Day, more catalogues, a

38

circular about classroom assistants. He skimmed through this last one until his eyes caught the words 'reduction of hours'. He read it properly, then swore out loud. They were cutting the hours of classroom assistants – 'an unwelcome but forced economy'. With a cringe he remembered his conversation with Mrs Craig. Hardly an auspicious start. Outside in the playground Eric was putting litter into a black polythene bag. He remembered the leak in her roof. It would scarcely compensate but it was better than nothing. When he rang Building Control in the Board he spoke to someone who asked him how big the hole was, what kind of roof it was, and how often the rain came through. The matter was considered more complex than he had anticipated, with the extent and potential cost of the repair determining which source of funding it would come from. If structural work was required, it would have to come out of 'new build' as opposed to minor works. There was a prioritised waiting list. Someone would have to come out and inspect the roof. When would that be? There was a backlog, difficult to say. He could feel his affability slowly fading. He needed to be able to give Mrs Craig some form of compensation, but there was no sense of urgency at the end of the phone, only a lukewarm concern and no indication of any immediate action. Mrs Patterson came in with some forms and smiled as she listened to his increasingly frustrated attempts to hear the words he wanted.

'Not the easiest people in the world to stir,' she said a little smugly as he put the phone down. 'Quicker to buy a bigger bucket.'

In the playground infant classes were being released. Young mothers came through the gates to collect their children. Some skipped forward with their arms outstretched, others stood more cautiously by the gates and waited, shopping bags clutched in their hands. He had lost track of time. Soon it would be the staff meeting. He scribbled a few notes on the back of an envelope but he knew already the things he was going to say. Outside in the street there was the sound of car engines starting up, the slamming of doors.

His own mother had come to collect him on his first day in school. His class had come out in twos, hand in hand, their heads straining to see who was waiting for them. Someone had shouted, someone had dropped hands and was running. Everyone was running. A red apple, not a hard green windfall, bitter to the tongue, but a red apple bought from McMinn's fruit shop – that was what his mother had held in her hand. She had almost taken it back off him when she discovered the rosettes of paint on his clothes. The memory was like a little polished stone in his collection, something he had picked from the beach and stored safely. How big that first room had seemed as it hunched over him with its high, small-paned windows through which only sky could be seen, how stern Miss Winters had seemed in her stiff white blouse with the turquoise brooch at the collar. Her name always made him think of snow and frost. And now he had returned, drawing a fine, full circle of his life. The inadequacies of the day drained away. He remembered the children at play, flowing round him, the sunlight through the bars washing over their faces, and he was filled with a new sense of optimism.

*

After giving the staff five minutes to clear up and grab a quick cup of coffee he entered the staffroom. Mrs Haslett had obviously made some comment about the circular arrangement of chairs and others were staring at them as if they represented some kind of threat. Miss Fulton stood cupping her coffee in her hands, obviously unsure of where to sit. He made a joke about how he was glad to see that everyone appeared to have survived. It interested him to see that Vance and Haslett sat together in the seats across from him. No one sat on the chairs on either side of him and he used them to stack his handouts.

As he ran through the new administrative arrangements, Miss McCreavey and Miss Fulton made notes in the back of their diaries. Vance sat quietly, his eyes fixed somewhere on the opposite wall, while Haslett stared at him in a way that said she was inspecting him rather than listening to what he was saying. His own eyes lingered briefly on her shoes – green patent leather with insets of white triangles and gold stitching. In a silent pause as he passed out the handouts, he could hear the clink of Eric's mop bucket as the mop head rattled the handle and then the slushy squeak as it slithered across the wet tiles.

He led them through the pages, outlining proposed changes demanded by the Education Reform Act, explaining the working parties he was setting up to evaluate their school curriculum. He tried to take a pragmatic course, expressing his own doubts about aspects of the changes – the usual lack of training and resourcing, the burden of assessment – but also tried to encourage them to be positive in their response.

He glanced up at the tight ring of faces and read their disquiet, their silent exasperation. Suddenly the physical distance which separated them from him seemed to stretch further, and he felt increasingly ill at ease and disjointed in his speech. He paused as his line of thought rushed blindly into a dead-end and through the breach caused by his hesitation flooded their incredulity and all the questions for which he had no easy answers.

What did you do with thirty other children when one was being assessed? When were they supposed to find time for all the paperwork? What would pages of ticks in boxes tell you about a child's ability?

Fiona Craig said things he agreed and sympathised with and it made him feel uncomfortable to be placed in the role of spokesman for the government, an apologist for policies devised by civil servants. In the face of her passion and frustration he knew he sounded mealy-mouthed and unconvincing, but he tried to steer his middle course, suggesting compromises and shortcuts, trying as always to talk from a teacher's perspective. He felt more and more defensive, under pressure.

Mrs Haslett, smelling blood, increasingly pushed in for her share, her eyes wide behind her glasses and her head nodding slightly as she took her bite. 'I wonder what Mr Reynolds would have made of all these changes? Given them short shift I expect.'

'I think Mr Reynolds took early retirement precisely because he knew there was no way these changes could be avoided.' He paused, his own frustration rising, and scanned the circle. 'Whether we like it or not this is the face of the future, and so long as it's on the statute book we have to find some way to work it.'

He knew he was slipping towards the type of confrontation he had been determined to avoid. He was saved only by Haslett's insistent attempts to dominate the discussion and the silencing of those with more perceptive perspectives. Inevitably she defended the status quo, made trite little points based on anecdote and prejudice, delivering them as if they were profundities. He replied calmly to each of them, patronising her each time by the cheerful use of her first name, letting the shots bounce off him, smiling at times, sometimes directing them back with a gently barbed question. She was running out of steam, out of support.

Vance had said little, content to make a few disparaging

comments about educational theorists, the transience of fashionable ideas when set beside the traditional solidity of what he described as 'sound teaching'.

Then Miss Fulton said something optimistic, oblivious to the withering glance. He could have hugged her. Miss McCreavey, too, said something supportive, and the tight power of the circle was broken. He made a joke – only Vance and Haslett did not laugh.

He had made it. At one point as the rapids jutted jagged and large ahead of him it had been in the balance, but he had not panicked and had steered a course through. Now that he was in calmer waters and the end of the meeting in sight, he went on the offensive and brought up the question of the entrance hall.

'Frankly, it depresses me. I'm sure together we could make it more inviting, use it to create a more positive impression of the school and the work that goes on in it.'

They looked at him impassively.

'I'm going to ask Eric to put up some display boards and I thought it would be a good start if we could all have our classes make a display for Hallowe'en – perhaps fireworks, autumn leaves, that sort of thing.'

'*All* classes?' asked Vance.

'Yes, all classes. We don't want anyone to feel left out.'

'P7 are very busy, as I'm sure you realise, with preparations for the Transfer Test.'

'I appreciate that, but a change of activity would be good for them.'

'Don't forget, Mr Cameron,' said Mrs Haslett, 'that since the Troubles fireworks have been banned and many of our children won't ever have seen any.' Her head quivered almost imperceptibly. It was clear she thought she had found an

Achilles' heel but he saw it only as a final, rather pathetic throw.

'Think of it, Muriel, as an exercise in imagination,' he said, smiling at her.

Before she could think of a response he thanked them for their time and attention, and as she attempted finally to say something her words were lost in the scraping of chairs and the opening of locker doors.

The corridors smelled of disinfectant and were still wet as he locked his office door. Hugging the side of the wall, he stepped as lightly as he could, but when he reached the general office he turned round to see his footsteps following him, grey prints of grime. He feigned a grimace to Mrs Patterson as she put on her coat. It had been a long day and he was glad to be going home.

As he took the ten minute drive down country lanes he felt strangely empty. The softening strands of light dulled the ragged blossoms of the hedgerows into a smear of sameness. Behind them, ridged backs of ploughed fields smacked into each other at awkward angles. A half-hearted attempt at a scarecrow lolled sideways, its stick arms bereft of clothes. As he drove on automatic pilot he saw a glimpse of the future – an arbiter of petty feuds, a dealer of small cards, an apologist for things he did not believe in. What should have felt like a beginning suddenly felt like the end of something.

On the skyline a tractor snail-trailed a line of shimmering sod. He slowed the car to take a corner. A gate into a field was half open and behind the metal bars was a child's face. It was the girl with the blonde hair. He waved his hand instinctively, but she dropped her eyes behind a bar, her knuckles clenching tightly. He looked back in his mirror, but saw only a flock of gulls falling like snow into an open field.

*

44

As he turned into the driveway of the house they had bought three months earlier, he had to brake hard to stop running into an emerging cyclist. Tom Quinn was a local handyman-cum-gardener who had done some work for them – a bit of re-plastering and pointing, replacing cracked roof tiles. They had also called him in on several occasions when their purchase of the former rectory had seemed like an act of reckless romanticism, rather than a sound financial investment. He got off his creaking bike and leaned in at the driver's window. He was in his late fifties with a tight cap of wiry grey hair and blue eyes light against the dark creases of his weathered face. His broad stubby fingers rested on the ledge as he shook his head slowly from side to side in a wordless expression of bewilderment.

'The septic tank again, Tom?'

'Aye, Mr Cameron, your wife called me this afternoon. I still can't fathom where it's coming from.' He drummed his fingers on the ledge. There were neat curves of cement under his fingernails.

They had noticed the smell several weeks after they had moved in – it seemed to seep slowly into the bathroom, barely noticeable at first, a faint scent of sewer, then gradually it inflated the whole room until it was stretched taut with a septic stink. They closed the door. There was a trace of it in the kitchen. Sometimes they imagined it in other parts of the house and went about sniffing like people with heavy colds, never sure if they themselves carried the smell into new rooms. Then, as suddenly as it came, it would disappear. They made jokes about the Amityville Horror house but the joke was beginning to wear thin.

'There's obviously something wrong with the tank, Tom. The system's not working somewhere.'

The heavy fingers rose and fell as if playing notes on a

piano. 'I don't understand it. I've had the manhole covers up and I can't see a blockage anywhere. Mrs Cameron flushed paper down and I watched it shoot through clean as a whistle. I put two new traps in the bathroom last week and sealed them, so I just can't see how the smell's getting back in.'

They both shrugged grimly at the unsolved mystery and then, as Quinn wheeled his bike out through the gate, he drove up to the house, the loosely-gravelled driveway scrunching and squirming under his wheels. Emma was standing in the doorway of one of the outbuildings, her T-shirt and cut-off jeans splashed with paint. She had pinned her hair up but a blonde wisp trailed forward like a question mark. She had sounded up in her phone call, but he could tell from his first glance that the mood had evaporated. As he walked towards her he was about to make some joke about flushing toilet paper but thought better of it. When she gave him her cheek to kiss he noticed the stipples of paint on her eyelids, and then without asking him about his day, she went in and gestured round the room with the paint roller. Two of the walls were now white but they looked rough and uneven and in need of more coats of paint.

'I wanted to get it finished today to have it done for you coming home, but by this afternoon the smell was back, as bad as ever. I asked Mr Quinn to come over. He's very nice but I don't think he knows what to do. I've spent half my day flushing yellow toilet paper down the loo and shouting out of the bathroom window but I don't think he's any the wiser.'

'I know, I spoke to him at the gate.' He looked round the half-painted room. 'It'll be good when it's finished,' he said, trying to cheer her up, but the words sounded trite and unconvincing.

The couple of outhouses were one of the features which had attracted her to the house. She wanted to turn one into a studio for her art work and he had encouraged her, encouraged anything which would keep her busy and positive. During the summer they had installed new windows, opening it up to good natural light, and fitted some electrical heating so she would be able to work in the winter. But now she slumped on to a wooden chair and watched as the roller she was holding dripped gently on the newspaper-covered floor. For a few seconds he felt resentful of her, begrudging the time and energy he would have to invest in restoring her to better spirits. It should have been his day for special attention, some gentle pampering to ease away the stresses of a new job, but she was slipping further into herself, and for the few moments it took to fight off his disappointment the only sound was the steady splat of paint on to newsprint.

As more months went by, sometimes he could not help thinking her selfish. She was so self-absorbed, preoccupied with her own pain that it left no room for an acknowledgement of his, an unspoken assumption that the loss was entirely hers. It had been a boy. She had carried him for four months, losing him without warning in one of those moments that convinced all those without the comfort of faith that fate chose often to be both personal and malevolent. They had tried for a child for a long time with no apparent reason for earlier failure. Perhaps it was always this way whatever the circumstances. He preferred to shut it away in that part of himself which was hidden, just as he had packed away all the clothes and objects which were to have been for the child in an old suitcase, and lodged it in the darkest corner of the roof-space. He had placed them in the cheap brown case they had bought for their honeymoon, and stored it out of sight the night before she had come home from hospital. Jumpers his mother had knitted in the neutrality of lemon and white, their neat rows of tiny stitches small enough for some child's doll. A musical mobile with prancing circus horses. The goofy soft toy she had bought the day the doctor told her she was pregnant. Other bits and pieces they had gathered or been given by friends who no longer needed them. A memorial to something that had never existed except in the future images they had conjured and painted in the privacy of their imaginations. Alone in the house he had felt only a sense of numbness as he searched vainly for some emotion that was recognisable, or even appropriate, but there was only that clinging sense of coldness clasping him tightly, like the way the early morning mists layered the sleeping fields. He had tried to cry, tried to get drunk, but it felt too much as though he was acting out a part in some cheap film, smacked too much of self pity. Perhaps it would have been better if she had seen him cry, maybe then she could have shared her own pain more openly, rather than hugging it tightly to her like a phantom child. But he knew he could not have cried in front of her because to do so would have altered the way he thought about their relationship. She was the fragile one, he the stronger, and the evidence of his love for her was the responsibility he assumed for her well-being. She was like one of his children, entrusted into his care forever through a ceremony and the exchange of rings.

He knelt down beside her and eased the roller out of her hand, then rested it on the paper. 'I'll be able to help at the weekend. It'll not take long to get it in shape with two of us working at it.'

'I wanted to have it finished for you coming home, but it's a bigger job than I thought — the walls don't take the paint very well.'

He took her hand and felt the paint stick their palms together. 'After you've finished I want you to bring your magic roller and give the school the once-over — staff included. Everywhere and everyone from top to bottom.'

He coaxed her now, eased her out of her depression by talking to her about his day, making things seem funny, exaggerating and colouring, leaving out the bits that lingered even now like a bad taste on his tongue. He wanted to tell her about assembly and the rows of sun-washed faces, about break and the undulating waves of play but knew he did not have the words, and was unwilling to risk damaging the few warming memories he had salvaged from the day.

Things would get better. She herself had instigated the idea of buying a house in the country, of leaving their suburban Belfast semi and the social set she had lost interest in. At that time he had gone along with all her ideas – giving up her administrative job in the Arts Council, going back to her painting, setting up a studio and small gallery at home. Even if it did not work, in the long run it would occupy her time and energy, help salve the pain.

Inspired by months of looking in magazines devoted to soft-focussed pictures of country life, all washed in a kind of pastel-coloured pastoralism, she had plumped at first sight for the old rectory, and he had been prepared to subdue his more prosaic concerns about practical matters with the knowledge that the price was reasonable, and the location brought him back to his old heartland. Familiar territory carried with it a feeling of security, of re-entering that safe world he identified with his childhood, and if sometimes it made him uneasy to think of how close the rectory was to a darker place in his past, he shrugged it off. Really the only doubt in his head was whether she would sustain her new-found enthusiasm for country living. As much as she loved his mother, she had always found anything longer than a short stay an obvious strain.

He thought of the first time she had met his family which, despite his best efforts, had assumed all the rituals of a formal introduction – best table-cloth and china, his mother bullying his father into his Sunday best, the dog ousted from the kitchen, his two older, bantering brothers dispatched to jobs in far-off corners of the farm. Even in the most subdued of her art college outfits she had looked startling amidst the staid and sombre tints of the parlour. He remembered the gaping lulls in the conversation, extenuated by the ponderous tick of the clock, his father's persistent rubbing of his finger round the rim of a tight collar. Just when he was worried they would mistake her quiet self-containment for something worse, his mother had taken her into the kitchen. He had strained in vain to hear what was being said over his father's insistent poking of the fire, the rustling of his newspaper, the gush of water into a kettle. And then, through a side window, he saw them walking in the garden, his mother linking her arm and pointing across the field. They both were laughing.

'Aye well that's that then,' his father had said, glancing up from the paper, relief evident in his face. A few minutes later the paper dropped to the floor and he headed off to find his working clothes.

His mother's open acceptance of her helped to bridge the gap between their two families but could never totally blur the distinctions. She was an only child of well-off parents who had sold their family business, taken early retirement and spent their time playing golf or enjoying frequent holidays abroad. Affable, generous parents but a world away from his own background. He got on well with them and listened politely to their advice about good investments even when he didn't have two pennies to rub together. Emma tried hard too, but never fully unravelled the intricate web of relationships which bound an extended rural family – the pecking order, the taboos, the standing jokes. She was a private, shy person and she found it hard to enter into the small-talk centred on local trivia which was the main medium of personal exchange. He knew several of his aunts thought she had 'airs and graces', but his mother understood her best and tolerated no open criticism.

They had been married for five years. She was six years younger than he was. There was still time to have children. They would try again and maybe they would get lucky. They had not made love since it had happened. She showed no sign of wanting anything other than the simplest forms of affection and he preferred to suppress his desires rather than appear insensitive. When he thought of sex it made him feel guilty, predatory.

By the time the evening meal was over and cleared away she had slipped into better spirits and asked him questions about his day. He hid all his negative feelings from her and was up-beat and optimistic in his responses, talking about Mrs Haslett and making her more of an ogress than she really was, sharing the intimacy of the creaking car seats. He told her about the missing jotters and as he talked his flippant, humorous tone soothed some of his own apprehensions. The future would be what he would make it. Everything would work out the way he had always conceived it.

As they walked in the garden together he listened with concealed amusement to her plans.

'I thought we'd have a mixed border in front of the hedge and a border sweeping up to the house with herbaceous plants – maybe shrub roses as well,' she said, gesturing with her hand as if focussing it in her imagination was enough to make it a reality. 'Do you think we should try to grow something up the front walls of the house?'

He nodded and suggested she should draw out her plans, translate some of her ideas into small sketches, but restrained himself from commenting on the potential cost of the practicalities involved.

Afterwards he did some school-work, reading some of the new proposals for assessment. They depressed him in the same way the school foyer or Haslett's classroom had depressed him. They were written in the language of the new mandarins, smugly self-confident, full of bland vagaries, an acronymic cant printed on glossy paper. He tried to wade through it, underlining sentences in fluorescent pen, wondering how he would be able to translate it into any kind of recognisable reality for his staff. But his mind grew increasingly tired and like wheels stuck in sand the words went nowhere, spinning endlessly round in his head. He found he had read the same paragraph two or three times without taking it in and he tried finally to focus his full concentration on it. Still it made no sense and the more he read it, the further removed it seemed to be from the world of teaching children.

Emma came into the study. She had been watching television. He put the marker down and stretched in the chair. She rested her arm across his shoulders and, glancing at the document he was reading, simulated a yawn of boredom, then kissed him on the top of his head and went on up to bed. He sat on for a few minutes before packing it all into his briefcase, then turned off the silent television she had been watching and went to check that the doors were locked. He stood staring out into the dusk for a few minutes. Years of city living had made him forget the peculiar patina of country light, the way the dark rolled in across the fields to beach soundlessly against the lines of the house, the feeling it brought of being isolated from the rest of the world but secure and solid in the sanctuary of the shadows.

A black pulse of speed quivered in the sky. A bat? The last swallow of summer? He was not sure, but it made him shiver and he locked the door and climbed the stairs to the bathroom. A bedside lamp shed an arc of light on to the landing. He entered, closed the door and sniffed. He could smell it, the faint septic scent, not pronounced or intrusive but lingering somewhere, hidden, waiting to unwind itself and filter silently into the vents and crevices of the house. If only they could find the source they would be able to do something about it. He got down on all fours and sniffed round the outflow pipe at the back of the toilet, his hand unwilling to touch the webbed and leprous skin of paint behind the washhand basin, around the tiled base of the shower. He felt like a dog sniffing round a lamp post but he kept going, lifting his head from time to time and holding it alert in the air. He moved up and down along the side of the bath and then, taking a screwdriver which Quinn had left on the window ledge, unscrewed the panel and looked at the new trap which had been fitted. He pulled at it gently but it sat snugly, wearing a tight collar of sealant. Then, screwing the panel back on, carefully using the same screws in the same holes, he stood up and dusted his knees.

When he entered the bedroom he could tell that his wife was already asleep. Turning off her light, he undressed in the dark and quietly got in beside her. He lay still and silent for a few moments then got up and went back to the bathroom. The cistern moaned and water spurted through buckled pipes. He closed the door tightly and went back to bed and hoped he would not dream.

*

'Mr Cameron, you understand that Mr Reynolds clearly promised me that I could have the use of the hall on a Friday afternoon. I don't know where Miss McCreavey got the idea that she had booked it.'

School had not started. Outside his window he could see the children being left off by their parents. 'Perhaps she got the idea from Mr Reynolds,' he suggested.

'But he clearly told me I was having it.'

He had to spell it out for her. 'Perhaps he promised the same thing to both of you.'

'Mr Reynolds wouldn't have done such a thing.' Her tone suggested that he had just accused her former headmaster of the grossest impropriety.

'I think, Mrs Haslett, we'll have to find some sort of compromise. You appreciate better than I do how limited space is.'

'Could Miss McCreavey not use her classroom?'

It was possible the conversation would stretch into infinity. He had better things to do – an assembly to prepare for a start. 'I'll tell you what, Muriel, leave it with me and I'll let you know by the end of school what's happening.'

Like a dog with its teeth in a bone, she seemed unwilling to let the matter go, but he'd had enough and, standing up from behind his desk, began to look through his filing cabinet. He did not turn round until he heard the door close behind her.

It was a poor start to the day and it set the tone of what was to follow. A clatter of post had subsided across his desk by the time assembly was over: two circulars from the Board; an update from the Curriculum Council; book publishers' catalogues; a brochure from a school travel company; a miscellaneous mess of advertising material; letters from parents. His whole morning seemed to be consumed by bitty fragments of administration that prevented him doing any of the things he had intended. He telephoned again about the hole in the roof and was told the matter was now in hand, but was given no assurance as to the date of completion. He had a difficult fifteen minutes with Mrs Craig when he broke the news about her classroom assistant, but promised that when financial delegation passed into the school's hands, he would make it a priority. She was unimpressed and he could not really blame her. She also pointed out that the mother who helped in that capacity might not find it financially worthwhile to continue in the job. She was paid little enough as it was.

A parent telephoned to enquire where she could purchase transfer tests for her eight-year-old daughter. Another, on the strength of a couple of lessons, queried the way Miss Fulton was teaching maths, pointing out that her methodologies seemed to be different from her predecessor. Some salesman wasted twenty minutes of his time trying to get him to agree to a demonstration of a colour photocopier which he knew he could not afford. Unannounced and without any coherent explanation, two men arrived from the Board's architects' department and proceeded to measure the school then ask technical questions about the building for which he did not have the answers. There was a query from someone in the pay branch about what hours Eric had worked during the six-week summer scheme. He felt increasingly frustrated, pushed from one petty task to the next. The only saving grace of the day was P7 history. It was his main subject and while Vance took Miss Fulton's class for music he would take P7 for their year's history. He had instructed Mrs Patterson that he was not to be disturbed during the lesson except in an absolute emergency, and as he entered the classroom as a teacher this time he felt as though he was finally pitching on home ground, back where he belonged.

He had planned to follow a unit of work springing from local history and centred on the Celts. It had struck him, too, that it was a project which would easily become part of the

EMU scheme, proposed by Liam Hennessy, with the two schools going on joint field trips to visit local sites. After showing the class slides of the Book of Kells he got them to decorate the covers of their history notebooks as ornately as they could. Emma had cut out stencils for him, including decorative lettering, so that even the weaker children were able to produce something that was pleasing to the eye. He got them to move their desks and work in groups of four. They used tinfoil and the insides of chocolate wrappers to create the impression of silver and gold leaf. They worked well for him, enjoying the novelty of the degree of freedom he offered, not bold enough yet to talk openly but whispering conspiratorially and looking at him guiltily to see if they had infringed some rule. And though he felt the urge to do something to free the children from the tight parameters which bound them, he knew he could not undermine Vance's relationship with his class, so he held himself in check, restricting himself to encouragement and a smile.

The smile faded as he walked to the back of the room. In his excitement and pleasure he had not noticed that the blonde-haired girl had joined no group but sat crouched over her desk, her arm curled round her book, hiding it from view. As he came down beside her the arm tightened round it, her head dropping lower. Playfully and gently he pulled at one of her locks but at his first touch she dropped her face into the book so that her cheek rested on the cover and her eyes stared away from him. He drew back his hand, startled and confused by a reaction he had not anticipated and struggled to interpret. Its suddenness, its defensiveness, shocked him, and for a few seconds he found himself unsure of what to do.

He went round to the other side of the desk and squatted on his haunches until his eyes were only about a foot away from hers. They were blue, bright, translucent, and in the corner of one was a tiny blear of mucus. She stared into his and did not blink. A blue pen mark ran across the paleness of her cheek like a varicose vein.

'What's your name?' he whispered, as if playing a game.

The eye closest to the desk blinked twice, a nervous involuntary pulse, but she did not speak. He did a funny smile at her but got nothing in return and then her lips moved almost imperceptibly and she was saying her name, so faintly he had to strain to catch it.

'Jacqueline.'

The three syllables came out as if they were only loosely connected and he heard the final two and guessed the first.

'Jacqueline.' Still on his knees, he repeated the name slowly.

Her tongue quickly touched her top lip before disappearing again. Standing up slowly, he asked her in the same whispering tone if she would show him her work. There was no response. He said please and then lightly moved her arm from its protective curve. It was stiff under his touch and in it he could feel the full weight of her reluctance. On the cover of her history book were a few scribbled attempts at decoration in yellow crayon and a faltering, slanted set of her initials. He was conscious that some heads were turned towards them and he sent them back to their work with a gesture of his hand. Only one face still stared.

'Sir, Jacqueline doesn't do the same work as us.'

'Thank you, Luke, now concentrate on getting your cover finished, please.'

He waited until the boy had returned to his work then pulled a chair alongside the girl's desk. There was a faint smell of urine. He coaxed her head off the desk and, taking the stub of pencil she had been using, turned her single-lined initials into two block capitals, then stencilled some decorative motifs into the four corners of the page. She still had said nothing other than her name, but he talked to her all the time, quietly, positively. He made her choose the colour of crayon she wanted to use for her initials and, seemingly without moving her eyes, she pointed to purple. Breaking the crayon in two, he gave her half and started to colour the J, motioning her to start the M. M for McQuarrie. He saw her name and address printed in an adult's hand on the inside of her plastic pencil case. He did not know the family but she lived on a road only five minutes' drive away from his own, and then he remembered having seen her at a gate on his journey home. She sat now, tongue pushing out her cheek and one leg swinging nervously. Sometimes she swung it too hard and it hit the leg of the desk and then she would glance furtively up at him to see if she had done something wrong. She coloured in the M, only occasionally slipping outside the lines, but shaded in different directions so that when she had finished it was an irregular patchwork. But he commended her and suggested some colours she could use for the stencilled decorations, then patted her gently on the shoulders and left her to work at it on her own.

Most of the class were putting the final touches to their work and he could see that they were pleased with the results. He conveyed his own pleasure to them and wound up the lesson early enough to leave time for packing up and returning the desks to their original positions. After the bell had rung he met Vance in the corridor. He was carrying sheet music and a metronome and looked surprised when his polite nod was returned with a request to step into his office.

'Jacqueline McQuarrie?' Vance flushed slightly. One of the copies of sheet music slipped forward in his hand but when he spoke his voice was matter-of-fact, almost disinterested. 'So you've met Jacqueline, then. Not a very satisfactory situation, I'm sure you'll agree.'

At that moment he did not feel like agreeing with anything Vance had to say. 'What exactly is the situation?'

'Jacqueline McQuarrie is . . . well, in the old days they would have described her as Educationally Subnormal. She has a reading age of about five or six and can only handle very basic number work. There's very few class activities she can join in with and really I'm not quite sure what I'm supposed to do with her. The only consolation is that her parents have opted her out of the transfer tests.'

He felt a sudden urge to swear, to grasp the metronome out of Vance's hands and bend it into a shape that would never beat time again. 'What is she doing here? She shouldn't be in this school. The child should be in a special school, or even a school with a special unit where there's staff trained to work with children like her, to give her the education she's entitled to.' He felt angry, as though he had just discovered something sick under his own roof.

'I'm sure you're right, Mr Cameron, but I don't think the blame lies with us. Her parents were advised by Mr Reynolds that she would be better off elsewhere but they chose to ignore it and insisted she came here. I wasn't privy to the discussion but they were quite adamant.'

In the middle of his anger there was still time to be irritated by the persistence with which Vance called him Mr Cameron, when he had been invited on several occasions to use his first name. His tone of voice was impersonal, his vocabulary formal. It was as though he had something stiff and unbending at his core, like a layer of permafrost – an absence of spontaneity, an unwillingness to reveal or share anything of his self.

'Mr Reynolds had no right to accommodate anything that was not in the best interests of the child and sticking her down at the back of the classroom could certainly not be described as promoting Jacqueline McQuarrie's welfare.'

'Perhaps there were other factors involved that you're not aware of.' His voice was distant now. 'You'll excuse me, my class are unsupervised at present.'

He waited a few seconds until Vance had left the office then smashed his fist down on top of the filing cabinet, indenting a hollow bruise in the metal. Pulling out the top drawer he searched through what passed for a record system. Under the girl's name he found a white card with her full name, address, date of birth and date of entry into the school. In a manilla file were copies of her last three reports but a cursory glance was enough to absorb the extent and nature of the information. Bare, perfunctory statements that the child experienced severe difficulties in all her subjects with no reference to personal and social development or any proposed course of remedial action. He sat down at his desk and turned the miserable, meagre information over and over.

His thoughts were disturbed by a now-recognisable knock on his door and the entry of Haslett. In her wake trailed a red-faced boy. It was obviously a hanging job and her expression clearly indicated that a guilty verdict had already been reached and that he was required to play the role of executioner. She stood with her arms folded across her bosom like a plumped pillow, while the boy's eyes flitted nervously round the office. He felt as if he should open the drawer of his desk and put on a black cap.

'Mr Cameron, this is getting out of hand and I think it's about time we let parents know it's not acceptable.' She looked curiously like an owl when she was angry, a spasmodic twitch pushing her glasses further up her nose, enlarging her eyes, her face pulled tight and white like a knot, the words bursting out bitterly in a rush of air. 'I don't know what parents are thinking of to allow it. Well, they've got another think coming if they think I'm going to allow it in my class.'

Drawing phalluses on his jotter, bullying, spitting gobs of phlegm, cursing – the options were limitless. Looking at the accused he couldn't decide the crime. It had to be serious, though.

'Take off your jumper, Mr McBriar, and show Mr Cameron what you propose to do P.E. in.'

The boy obeyed but nervousness made his hands clumsy and for a few seconds his head struggled to emerge from the blue sweat-shirt, making it look as though he'd already been beheaded. She tutted in exasperation and for a few seconds he thought she was going to yank it off, but at last the boy wriggled his way free, his hair standing up like stubble. Across his chest was a familiar face and the large message, 'My name's Bart Simpson, who the hell are you?' She quivered with new outrage. He struggled to suppress a smile. 'Leave this to me, Mrs Haslett. I'll deal with it.'

He ushered her back to her class and closed the door behind her.

The boy stood still, one arm of his sweat-shirt trailing the floor like a prehensile tail.

'What's your name?'

'Neil McBriar.'

'Well, Neil, your T-shirt certainly seems to have upset Mrs Haslett. Bart Simpson is a bit too rude for this school, perhaps you shouldn't wear it at school again.' Matter closed. The boy flattened his crown of stubble with an unconscious flap of his hand that looked like a salute. Down the corridor he heard Haslett's door close. 'Put your sweat-shirt on and keep it on, please, till you're home.'

Bart Simpson's flaming exclamation of yellow hair extinguished in the dark folds of the sweat-shirt. The boy fidgeted, unsure of whether he was supposed to go or stay.

'Neil, do you know Jacqueline McQuarrie in P7?'

'Yes, Sir.'

'And what do you know about her?'

The boy hesitated, unsure of whether he was about to be accused of further crimes. 'I don't do it, but people in her class say she's stupid, backward. Nobody plays with her and she doesn't bother with anybody.'

'Do people tease her?'

'Sometimes people call her names.' He hesitated, caught between a desire to be absolved of blame for the T-shirt and an unwillingness to seem like a squealer.

'What do they call her, Neil?'

'Well, sometimes – I don't do it, Sir – Smelly Gyp or Betty Poo. Things like that.' He screwed his face up in a pretence of pretending. 'Sometimes they call her Dumbo. Most people don't bother with her, though, because once her Da came up and scared some boys who were calling her names.

'Does she have any friends?'

'I don't think so, but she doesn't want any friends because she never bothers with anybody, even when they try to be friends with her.' The boy stood staring at the floor, increasingly uneasy as he realised that he was having a conversation with the headmaster.

He let the boy go, realising that he himself was late for Miss Fulton's class. He had promised to help listen to pupils read and organise them into ability groups.

When he arrived she had already started, the children sitting in circles, books held proudly like prizes, but even in the presence of her newness, her naïve enthusiasm, he felt a sour taste in his mouth which deadened the enjoyment of the children and made it difficult to concentrate on their reading. The singsong voice of the girl beside him seemed to mock him, her dramatised, exaggerated pronunciation rubbing against his growing feeling of flatness.

He had a sudden fear that there might be more skeletons locked in cupboards and at any moment one might spring out at him. He had inherited something that still belonged to Reynolds. It had his handprints everywhere, the way his mind worked, the way he saw the world, and it would take time and energy before he made it his own. For the first time he wondered if he could ever fully shake it loose from the fossilised firmness of that grasp. It was a brief doubt. It was just like the house they had bought – at least there they had the benefit of a surveyor's report and knew beforehand the extent of the inadequacies – which window frame was rotten, which wall needed re-pointing. Tins of paint, windows open to let light and air in, the furniture you were familiar with, the precious objects and memories you brought, and soon you claimed it, made it part of you. So it would be with the school. He had been foolish to think that it would happen so quickly or easily. He would have to work harder at it, give it a little more of himself.

Glancing towards where Miss Fulton was showing her circle a picture in a book, their eyes met and she smiled at him. He felt warmed into new optimism, conscious of the voices of the children reading, and remembered his own first public steps: the graded readers which Mrs Preston had doled out, forcing himself to ration the pages because finishing too quickly would mean a long wait before he was given a new one. Standing at the front of his class and reading from a book – he could not remember which one – and Mrs Preston, the woman who no one had a good word for, giving him sixpence as a reward for his proficiency. The girl's head opposite him pecked at the words like a little bird, one of her legs folded underneath her. He concentrated now totally on everything around him and only the children's shifted focus told him someone had entered the room.

He followed Mrs Patterson down the corridor. It was the Reverend Houston on the telephone, but it seemed to be nothing more urgent than a desire to confirm dates for the Board of Governors' meetings and when he would come to school to take assembly. There was an exchange of small talk and then he felt the tone of the conversation change.

'I believe, John, you told Mrs Rooney that the Girl Guides could have the school hall for their display.'

He sensed some kind of problem, but could not anticipate what it was. 'Yes, that's right.'

'Well, John, it's just that really those sort of decisions have to be made by the governors.'

'She said they'd used the hall last year. I assumed it was OK.'

'They did use it last year after the governors approved it. You understand that we get a lot of requests to use the school premises and we have to be careful just who we let it out to. In a small community like this it's very easy to cause offence by a refusal and it makes it worse if they can come back to you and say, "Well, so-and-so got it, why can't we?" '

'I apologise – I didn't realise life was so complicated.' He felt like a pupil who'd just got his homework wrong.

'Not to worry. Hope everything's going well for you.'

And then he was gone. He remembered George's description and hoped he had not just encountered what might prove to be another thorn in his flesh. While he was by the telephone he rang Emma but there was no reply and he assumed she was working in the outhouse. He intended to ring again during the afternoon but it, too, followed a shapeless sequence of fragmented administrative jobs which left him with a growing feeling of emptiness.

It was a pattern that the succeeding days and weeks established as a norm, and at times it felt not so much as if he was the driver of the school but rather a kind of mechanic whose job it was to keep the wheels turning smoothly, the person to whom people turned when something went wrong or some part of the system malfunctioned. At the end of the day he felt tired in body and mind but could not always give a coherent account of how he had spent his time. There was too much paper, he knew that with certainty, too many forms and too many documents, impossible to assimilate or reflect upon. The one plus was the children. They were receptive and lively but without street sus, that harder edge of city kids. It frustrated him that he spent so little time with them.

Jacqueline was the one problem child to emerge. It was possible, even probable, that there were others of various hues, but they still nestled undetected in the corners and crevices of the system. She was no longer frightened of him, but still unable to look at or speak directly to him. He had not yet decided what to do about her and before he made any moves he wanted to speak to Reynolds and find out as much of her background as possible. Despite all his instincts, it was important not to go charging in and risk more harm than good. What he was sure of, however, was that he would not allow the situation to continue a day longer than was necessary.

*

As arranged, Quinn turned up at nine-thirty on Saturday morning and they started to dig at the back of the house, following the line of the pipe from the bottom of the kitchen to the first manhole cover where it connected with the waste pipe from the bathroom. They had lifted the flags first, then dug with pick and shovel to make an impression in the gravelly ground, and while he tried to match Quinn's work rate, he realised with embarrassment that paper blisters were already forming across the tops of his palms. Then gradually, as the hole widened, there was room for only one to do the hard digging and he was occupied by clearing away the loosened earth. A shard of green glass glinted in the sunlight. Emma brought tumblers of lemonade and their hands left muddied prints on the glass. As they worked they both hoped that they were about to uncover the source of the problem, a discovery which would compensate for the labour, but when the pipe was finally uncovered it appeared uncracked, entering flush into the wall, and flowing cleanly into the main drain, its collar of cement intact. Quinn scratched his head and crouched down on his haunches, tiny beads of perspiration running down the sheen of his skin.

'I don't know,' he said. 'I just don't know, Mr Cameron, where the dickens it's coming from. The drains and pipes don't seem to be blocked or cracked anywhere. It's a mystery.'

It was his recurring phrase about the smell and his expression encapsulated all his bewilderment and frustration. As he stood up his boot shed its moulded image in clay. They stood on either side of the raised manhole cover and sniffed like wine tasters savouring a fine bouquet, but there was only the faintest trace of the offending smell. They covered up the pipe again and replaced the pavers. He did not know much about sewerage systems but he tried to throw ideas at Quinn, hoping that one might just jolt a solution.

'Maybe there's something wrong with the septic tank itself. Maybe it's just not breaking down the solids. Sometimes it seems as if the gas is pushing back up the pipes and the only place it can escape is back into the house.'

'Aye, but, Mr Cameron, how's it getting into the house? That's what I don't understand. The traps are all regulation and I put new seals round them, so I just don't know.'

They walked to the corner of the garden where the septic

tank was buried, and using a crowbar, Quinn levered up the lid and slid it slowly aside. He felt a twinge of embarrassment as they stared into the dark well of waste. As the escaping gases puffed up they turned their faces away.

'Sometimes,' said Quinn, returning his gaze to the black hole, 'washing machines can set them off. All that hot soapy water stirs up their insides.'

They stood staring into the circular darkness like eskimos at an ice hole, no longer knowing what to say or how to proceed. Emma made tea and they sat in the kitchen repeating the same ideas and confusions as if somehow repeating them might suddenly spark a solution. Emma aired her frustrations, saying that there was no point re-decorating the bathroom if there might have to be major work done to it. Later, as Quinn was leaving, he told them to call him the next time the smell appeared and in the meantime they should try contacting the council's Environmental Health Department.

They spent the rest of the day working in the outhouse finishing off the painting and putting up shelves and the curtains she had sewn herself. They measured the floor to get an estimate for tiles and late in the afternoon the new carpet arrived for the hall and stairs of the house. There was a shared feeling that things were beginning to take shape, slowly falling into place.

After tea it was still warm enough to sit outside for a while. The south-facing view had been another of the house's attractions. It stretched unbroken and uninterrupted by other dwellings across the tented triangles of fields, stitched in place by the straight seams of hedgerows and trees. The house was on a raised site and so commanded a perspective that drew the eye into it, shuffling new glimpses with each new focus – the dark smudge of a house, a slow spiral of smoke, a tractor working a field. Directly opposite them the sloping hedgerow, already beginning to tint itself, marked the hidden line of the disused railway line which once linked provincial towns. In the distance the slumbering shape of the Mournes stretched supine and still. They sat feeling good, the satisfaction brought about when work has earned a rest. He reached across and took her hand, startled as so often by the thinness of her fingers, the way her wedding ring slipped on touch. For a second he thought of saying something to her but he did not have the words clear in his head and would not risk fragmenting the calm which had settled over the moment.

'What are you thinking John? Right now, what are you thinking?'

The suddenness and directness of her question startled him, sending him scurrying for some safe but convincing response. But he hesitated too long and knew she would think he was searching for some half-truth.

'It must've been some terrible thought if you can't tell me,' she teased.

He fumbled awkwardly for an escape. 'I don't suppose I was thinking much of anything really, apart from how lucky we are to have a view like this.'

She pushed him lightly with her shoulder. 'You're such a liar. Sometimes I think there's a whole world going on inside your head that you don't want me to know about. You don't have another woman tucked away somewhere do you?'

'I can't keep one woman happy, what would I want two for?'

Down below, an arrow-head of birds quivered slowly across the sky.

'You find it easy to be happy John, don't you? Whatever goes on in your head keeps you safe from things. You should teach me how to do it.'

The lightness had gone out of her voice. He didn't want the day to end like this. He felt a sudden urge to tell her

68

about his dreams, to let her know he suffered too, but he suppressed it and tried to shift the conversation towards future plans for the garden. He was in mid-sentence when she stood up and walked back to the house and although he called after her she kept on walking.

*

That night as they lay in bed he was alert and sensitive, tuned to receive the slightest signal she might give him in the shift of her body, the light brush of her hand, but she finished reading her book and curled herself like a question mark, hugging the pillow to her head. He lay awake until her rhythmic breathing told him she was asleep. He felt restless, his mind like some bird circling the events of the week, swooping to peck at painful moments.

He slipped out of bed and found his slippers in the gloom. She lay, a soft foetal shape in the bed, somewhere far away from him. On the landing the bare floorboards creaked, polished knots and silver-headed nails gleaming like eyes in the half-light. He remembered when his mother finally persuaded his father to have the house re-carpeted. He could see it clearly with its great floral swirls of red and yellow. She had been so proud of it that for the first few months she had covered the hall floor with cloths when the incursive sun sneaked in through the glazed front door. The past was always protected, neat, tidy, like the armchairs and sofa covered with the starched white antimacassars, the china cabinet with delicate plates and tiny glass ornaments. A fixed, safe world, bound by rule and road and if you played inside them everything would be all right, no harm would ever befall you.

Something took him to the attic. His eyes had grown accustomed to the dark. The door whined as he opened it but he calmed it with the touch of his hand. All around him sheltered the type of junk that people accumulated, the burrs that stuck unknowingly to the fabric of your life; things which were once important in their old home but had not yet found a place or a useful role in their new one. And there, too, although he could not see it behind the pile of newspapers and tea-chests, squatted the cheap suitcase bought for their honeymoon.

He closed the door gently and, staying close to the wall, quietly descended the stairs. Something about the house suddenly felt claustrophobic and he wanted to be outside, to drink the cool cleanness of the night air.

As he stepped outside it felt as if he was diving into a deep pool of silence, each step he took breaking the surface of the stillness. He stood for a few moments under the scree of stars, and then as the coldness began to seep into his body, turned to re-enter the house but stopped dead in his tracks as from across the fields drifted a high, pitiful wail. It echoed itself in an eerie cadence of lamentation. He felt his fear rising and then almost immediately an equal mixture of relief and foolishness as he recognised the sound he had not heard for many years. It was the cry of a fox, probably somewhere along the old railway line. And then, as suddenly as it had come, it was swallowed by the silence of the night, but as he slowly climbed the stairs to their bedroom it coiled itself round his head like wire.

*

A week later he called with Reynolds on the way home from school and found him in the garden. He was pruning shrubs, a pair of secateurs in one hand and the scrag-ends of summer bedding in the other. He came towards him across the freshly cut stripes of lawn like a figure on a chessboard. His face carried the mark of holiday sun and although he removed his glove and offered his hand in greeting, his eyes were curious, even suspicious.

'Just tidying up before the weather gets a chance to change.'

'You look like you got the benefit of your holiday.'

'Yes, very pleasant, though Paris is getting very expensive.'

Neither of them knew whether to use the other's first name, and they exchanged a few more minutes of small talk before he revealed the purpose of his visit.

'I'd like to talk to you about Jacqueline McQuarrie, if I may. I don't want to keep you from your gardening, but perhaps you could help me.'

For a few seconds Reynolds stared blankly at him as if struggling to recall the name from a long-closed file and then he nodded his head to show that he remembered the child under discussion.

'She obviously should be in a special school or a school with a special unit. I was wondering if you could fill me in with some background.'

Reynolds shuffled the dead stalks against his thigh and brushed some husks off the front of his bodywarmer. 'Jacqueline's an unfortunate case as you've obviously found out, but I'm surprised Kenneth Vance didn't fill you in on the circumstances. I think I discussed it with him at the time.' He paused and for a moment it seemed as though he had nothing more to say. 'We realised from the start of course, the child couldn't cope, but there wasn't a lot we could do.'

'You spoke to the parents?'

'Yes. I had Mr McQuarrie in and discussed it with him but he was of the opinion that it was best for his daughter to stay where she was.'

'Best for his daughter?'

71

'Yes, that's what he felt and after offering my professional advice there was little more I could do about it.'

'Did you ask the educational psychologist to assess her?'

'That wasn't possible. Her parents wouldn't give permission.' He put one of the rubber gloves slowly back on his hand and the gesture said the conversation had become tiresome to him. In the front window of the bungalow Reynolds' wife stood watching from behind the curtain. 'I think she got some peripatetic help for a while, but I don't suppose it made much difference.'

He looked at Reynolds' bare hand holding the secateurs with its raised tributary of veins, the spreading brown stipples, and the anger he felt inside melted into indifference and a desire to be gone. As he drove away his last view was of a stooped figure shovelling the husks of summer into a black polythene bag.

*

Crying softly, almost a whimper, so soft at first that he is not even sure if it's real or a trick of his imagination. Somewhere far off in a distance beyond time, somewhere inside the layered labyrinth of grainy light which crackles and spits like static. But it grows louder, more insistent, calling again and again, a rhythmic pleading which fastens to his brain and can't be shaken off. Now, shadowy, disconnected shapes drift in front of his eyes. He blinks, tries to push them aside to see more clearly but they re-form and block his way. What is the distance which separates them? Sometimes it changes – a long, unlit corridor of locked doors, a flight of bare stairs spiralling round a dark well, a laneway hemmed in by thorned hedges. But no matter how much he tries to force his way to the crying child the distance always remains the same. Opaque pulses of light flicker fiercely like a television screen trapped between stations. He tries to focus on the shifting source but stumbles blindly into the sleet of tears. They sting his face. He throws up his hands to protect his eyes. Now his myopic groping grows more desperate because the child calls to him by name. Louder, louder, calling from some amorphous world beyond his reach. Briars whiplash across his face but he stretches out his arms into the receding pool of greyness. If only he could reach its hands, grab hold of the tiny frightened fingers, he could pull it free, pull it into the light of the world. But the more he reaches out, the more the voice slips away into some swirling void. He staggers to its edge, calling out himself now in a quivering voice which skims across the surface of the darkness and then sinks like a stone. And then he, too, is falling, falling . . .

Into consciousness and Emma shouting at him and shaking him, pulling his head down to her and cradling him tightly. He was still trembling and he could feel the dampness of his sweat sticking to his skin. She was talking to him, calming him, but even as he regained control, began to feel foolish, he still clung to her. Then she was stroking his hair and when she asked him what it had been about, he made up a crazy story and pretended to laugh at his foolishness. But as he curled his body around the contours of hers and waited for sleep to come, he tried to shut away his secret, and as she slipped back into sleep he put his arm around her waist and buried his face in the small of her back.

*

On the Sunday morning he had the grass cut before Emma had surfaced. In the country you did not cut grass on a Sunday, but it was early and only a single car had gone past the house.

They were not churchgoers and it seemed silly to pretend to observe others' pieties. There was still a dampness on the grass beading the blades and sometimes the mower sprinkled a tiny spray of water on his shoes. There was, too, a freshness in the morning air and a calm which softened the mechanical repetition, and he experienced the pleasure of concentrating on nothing but the work.

After breakfast he still felt the urge to be outside and Emma agreed to join him for a walk. The morning sky was seared with pink and the day felt as if it held the final moments of summer, giving him a desire to use it, to drain the last drops of warmth from it, and as they walked along the narrow roads between the thick wedges of hedgerow he felt almost happy. Sometimes a car passed and they would move into single file or stand safely on the verge. People going to church, their Sunday best making them sit stiffly in their seats, exchanging waves, a nod of the head. Two horses cantered to a gate and stuck their heads over the top bar, their eyes soft yolks of curiosity. Emma pulled grass from the bank and fed them, cautious of their champing teeth, and he teased her about her nervousness.

Further down the road they came to a bridge which crossed the old railway line and they slipped between the end of the stone parapet and hedge and clambered down the slope leading to the track. The steep banks on each side were a tangled scrub of bush and trees while at the top tall hedgerows disguised the line's very existence. There were no sleepers, no metal debris anywhere to mark the line of the track, only the raised ridges of grass stretching like steps into the distance. It was a sanctuary for wildlife, birds, and in the soft sandy slopes was sprinkled a maze of rabbit warrens. Probably the fox was there somewhere, too.

They walked along the line, skirting the marshy stretches

where water seeped down the steep sides and soaked into pools of brackish water. In wet weather parts would be impassable. Whole sections had been almost reclaimed by the undergrowth and he had to push a way through, carefully holding branches open like a door so that they would not spring back into her face. Everywhere were secret covens of foxgloves fading into withered shadows of themselves, and festering blisters of toadstools. Sometimes they were startled by a sudden scurrying in the middle of some bush or a bird taking off from a branch overhead and then they had to stop and smile at each other to dispel their unease.

They walked along the line for about a mile, sometimes having to climb over rickety barriers erected by farmers who wished to discourage trespassers, and once they went under another bridge where the decaying innards of some discarded engine lay rusting under choking tendrils of ivy. When they came to a point where a solid barrier of barbed wire prevented further progress, they climbed the twisting ribbon of path which successive feet had worn to bare soil and emerged in a humped scrub of field.

They paused to regain their breath after the steepness of the climb and she pulled a burr from his hair. He was not sure where they were and it felt good, as if they were on some childhood adventure together. Walking to the top of the rise they looked about them to gain their bearings and she was talking to him, holding on to the sleeve of his jumper in mock exhaustion, but he was not listening, her words drifting through his senses. Down below, the copse of tall trees, the snake of stream beyond them. The angle where the hedgerows hit the curve of the road. A topography lodged in his memory. But it was the house, the house above all with its slate roof, squatting on the sweep of field under the shadow of the tree, whose pollarded branches clutched the sky like stumps of fingers. His eyes moved slowly from the line of the house to the stone barn and then away again. He crouched down almost as if he was frightened the house might see him, know that he had come back.

She was looking at him now, asking him what was wrong, her face searching for answers.

'Maguire's place – that's it. That's where it happened.'

He stood up and stared at it, his memory and the present fusing in a fleeting pulse of fear. He felt her hand slip into his. There was a tightness in his stomach. He had always known that the return to his home ground would eventually bring him to this place but he had always thought he would choose the time, never thought of it happening like this – unprepared, suddenly thrust at him when he did not expect it.

The place held them both still and silent. She pulled his hand, inviting him to return the way they'd come but he did not move, did not take his eyes from the house below.

'I want to look.'

'Are you sure?'

He didn't reply, but started down the slope to where the farmhouse nestled in the hollow. Everything seemed smaller, less solid than he remembered it, the different parts which went to make it disconnected and insubstantial. There was no smoke now from the house. He remembered there had always been smoke from the chimney and with it the smell of peat, a tight funnel which spiralled back towards the trees and then seemed to hang motionless, trapped in some depression. They walked across the fields from which she had made a bare living by renting out the land for grazing, and from what vegetables grew in the stony patch to the side of the house.

By now they could see the house was derelict, thin cordons of ivy fanning across the slate roof and black squares in some of the window frames where the glass was missing. A ragged tumble of tall grass and weeds smothered the garden, reaching the top of the broken fence, and clumps of gorse had crept closer and closer to the house.

After she had been released she had moved away. People said she had gone to England but no one knew for sure. It had briefly passed into the hands of someone else and then he, too, was gone, the land sold and the house left to rot. The wooden door, still the dark red he remembered, sagged inwards, held now by a solitary rusted hinge. They paused at the brick path which led up to the house. It felt as though he was about to step into his past but there were none of the feelings that normally brought, only a powerful surge of emptiness, a kind of trembling inside him which made him nervous and uncertain. Emma moved closer but suddenly he wished she was not there, did not want her to see or be part of this moment, but it was too late now and he had to go on.

He stepped out with a boldness he did not feel and made towards one of the windows. The little paint left on the sill was blistered and bubbled, flaking away at his touch. Resting his arms on it, he shaded his eyes from the reflected light and peered into the room. Empty of furniture, a light fitting hung limply from the low ceiling and on the fireplace was a fantail of smoke-blackened bricks. He looked at the faded pattern of wallpaper, its corners flapping loose with years of damp, and the black-framed mirror whose silvered surface stared into a cracked emptiness. The mirror in which each day she would have brushed her hair and pinned up the coil of tresses, the mirror where her fingers would have traced the lattice of lines spreading slowly from the corners of her eyes as she searched for signs of approaching middle age. Where, too, her secret slept, waiting to rise up and meet her unbroken gaze.

*

He climbed the tree carefully, selecting his hand- and foot-holds like an experienced climber while the scent of bark and sap swamped his senses and his hands felt sticky with resin. Once he reached the lower branches the hardest part was over and he sat in the fork and rested. His knees bore the crinkled print of bark and he tried to lick the resin off his hands. Above him the canopy of leaf and branch rustled in the breeze, light squinting through the moving mesh.

His eyes suddenly caught the scuffmarks on his sandals and he spat on them, then rubbed them with the cuff of his jumper. They were still new enough to merit regular inspections from his mother and he did not want to incur her wrath. He knew they had been expensive. They had gone the previous Saturday to Dawson's in Market Street in a kind of yearly ritual which marked the coming of summer, and Mr Dawson had measured his feet in the metal shoe with the sliding toes, then produced a green box from the steeply-tiered shelves. He had the habit of holding the box in his broad hand and removing the tissue with a flourish to reveal the shoes as if performing some conjuring trick.

When they were on his feet, Mr Dawson pinched the toes with his thumb and finger to assuage his mother's concern that there was growing room, and he had to parade the length of the shop, conscious of their eyes on his feet. A serious business buying shoes. He loved the smell of the new leather, the cleanness of the white spongy sole, but above all he loved the lightness on his feet. After the clumpy heaviness of his black winter shoes, it felt as if his feet had sprouted wings, like he was walking on air. It was difficult to resist the impulse to run but that would have to wait until he was on his own. Mr Dawson parcelled his old shoes in the green box. On Monday the tissue would wrap an apple he took to school and later the box would be used to store the newest recruits to his model army. On their way out his mother would give him the pennies from her change to drop into the collecting box held by the lifesize model of a boy with callipers on his legs, the boy with blue eyes and pleading face who stood sentinel in the shop doorway.

It had begun with shoes. It must have been the lightness of his step that carried him further that day. It was May and the lanes were white with cow parsley in the verges and hawthorn blossom in the hedgerows. White like a wedding cake. He was often alone as a boy but rarely lonely, and that Saturday he knew no other restriction but the extent of his own impulse, and on this day it carried him outside the normal parameters of his play. There was a feeling, a scent of summer which gave him a sense of freedom, a desire for newness in his wanderings and so he followed the stream, its soft voice where it lisped and splashed over stones his only companion. Followed it as it dawdled and curved round the reeded banks and pock-marked edges where cows had stood to drink. Clouds of midges trembled and sometimes a dragonfly skimmed its surface. He dropped a peeled stick into the water and followed its voyage but soon its pace was too slow and boredom made him leave it becalmed in still water. For a second he thought of stepping on stones along its shallow stretch but remembered his sandals and could not risk the telltale white marks.

Across the fields now which were new to him, and then he saw the copse. It was almost circular in shape, clumped on a slightly raised plateau, its circumference bound by a moat of bushes and a yellow flame of gorse so bright it hurt his eyes. With little effort his imagination fashioned it into a fort, a walled castle which invited exploration and so he followed the narrow path which wound its way into its heart. It was darker now and the dappled light filtering through the meshed vault of branches reminded him of the way light seeped through

79

the coloured glass of church windows on Sunday morning. A secret world of sky and shadows, and he knew from the start that it would be a special place. He touched the trees as he walked, as if by touching them he gave them names and claimed them for his own.

To his disappointment he broke into a clearing where the blackened bones of a fire showed that someone else knew this place, but he told himself that it had been a tramp, or travelling person who was long gone and would never return. He pushed his way through brambles which plucked at his jumper, holding his hands high in the air as if wading through water, and made his way to the other side where it broke open revealing the world below. He climbed a tree, the one he was to climb again and again, then made his way along a knotted branch which jutted out into space, sitting astride it and shuffling his way forwards until he reached a point where he could peer through the veil of leaf and see the countryside spread out before him. See, without being seen, the house below while all about him the trees rustled and breathed gently.

A house with a red door and a blue slate roof. A curl of smoke. A yard with a stretch of flapping washing held aloft by an angled wooden pole; a piled store of peat; a stone barn to the side of the house. He saw her too, working a hoe in the vegetable patch with its ridged rows, stooping from time to time to pick out a stone or weed. Her hair was pinned up and sometimes she stopped to push a fallen wisp of hair from her eyes. Her name was Maguire – he had been in McMinn's fruit shop one day when she had placed a box of lettuce on the counter and Mr McMinn had marked the transaction in a ledger he kept under the counter.

Once she stopped for a rest and glanced up at the trees, looked right at him, but he knew she could not see him and it made him feel like a god, as if he had power over her, and at the same time his feeling of omnipotence was tinged with guilt, an awareness that he was spying on her. He meant no harm but her world was open to him, drawn into his vision like light into an eye.

It became a game, this journey to the copse, nestling in the sanctuary of the branches and watching the world below. He became familiar with her movements, came to recognise the clothes she wore and grew intimate with the pattern of her work. Always only a game.

As May slipped into June he found himself spending more time in his secret place but he told no one about it, afraid that to share its existence would rob him of its ownership. He made a makeshift hide and stored objects which he surreptitiously borrowed from home. He watched her build a scarecrow and drape it with tattered clothes, watched her move through the repetitive pattern of her life, as she tilled the flinty ground that was greening with new growth. And never any visitors, just once a younger woman on a bicycle who stayed a short while and then was gone.

Only one thing eluded him, one thing for which he found no meaning. At intervals she would walk to the stone barn. Usually she would carry some sort of container, a bowl perhaps, and then return a few minutes later. He could tell by the way she held it then that the bowl was empty. Wooden pallets and sacking blocked the windows and the slated roof was mottled with yellow moss. A bowl of meal perhaps. She always paused before entering and then one day, in the glint of light on metal, he knew that it was to unlock the door with a key. Perhaps she was frightened someone would steal her stock, or maybe it stored something valuable to her, but it was a small thing and it drifted to the back of his mind.

Once his mother mentioned her in a conversation he overheard, only a passing reference that told him little, other than that she was a widow whose husband had died in an accident ten years earlier, and she had a grown up daughter living in England. That was all anyone seemed to know. One Saturday he saw her for a second time in the town, scurrying with her busy, anxious gait. She walked right past him, a canvas shopping bag clutched in her hands. He looked into her face and for the first time saw the features which had always been just too far away to grasp. He did not know what age she was but maybe about the same as his own mother, with a small tight mouth and dark brown eyes that seemed to burrow deep into her head. She wore a long green raincoat, belted and buttoned tightly about her, and her shoes were scuffed and splashed with mud. Her hair was pulled back tightly and pinned in a bun and it made her face look pinched and taut. As they passed, he half-expected her to look at him and recognise him, but instead she stared straight ahead. He watched her hurry down the street, never pausing to look in shop windows, separated from everything around her, like a shadow moving across a field.

Now the grass grew tall, fanning in undulations, allowed to grow before being cut for silage, while in the trees leaves thickened and blocked out more light, casting flitting, trembling shadows which darted about him like fish in a rock pool. The sap of summer was in the touch and smell of everything. Soon school would end and bring the possibility of new adventures. And as that day approached he grew more curious about the stone barn and the journeys she made with the bowl. Slops to feed some animal or poultry? But why were they never allowed outside? How could they live in the dark outhouse where only slivers of light would filter through the cracks in the wooden pallets? He thought, too, of the key with which she opened and locked the door. What was it that she was so frightened of people stealing?

Gradually he grew bored with his game, frustrated with a life where nothing happened, and he knew he would soon desert it. Then, one Saturday afternoon when he had fled the visit of aunts, he saw her come out of the red-painted door, her canvas bag in her hand and wearing her belted raincoat. He knew she was going into town.

He watched her hurrying down the laneway on to the road, her pinned-up hair bobbing above the top of the cut hedgerow, and on impulse he was down the tree and walking across the field, the seeded heads of grass lapping round his waist. He hesitated for a second at the fence, then climbed over it, the wooden post trembling for a second under his weight then vibrating slightly as feelings of guilt rustled inside him. No one would know. Just one look at everything to see it clearly, cleanly, like the final focus of a lens, and then he would be gone forever. No harm to anyone, just the final satisfying of a curiosity and then forgotten. His hand on the whitewashed walls of the house, baked warm by the sun, his shadow moving in front of him like a ghost.

He came to the window but could not bring himself to do anything but glance guiltily out of the corner of his eye and move on, almost as if to stop and stare would be to intrude too deeply. He glanced at his fingers whitened with dust like chalk and as he faltered across the front of the house he carried an image of a brown interior like a sepia photograph. A mirror on the far wall, a crackling square of frizzling light. Into the yard and saw for the first time the lopped branches of the trees piled on top of each other, one of them stretched across a cutting block, an axe buried in the rotting bark, the yellowed end of the branch broken off like a snapped pencil. The heaped mound of peat, two sheets on a clothes line, a wooden pole with a V cut in its end holding them up like a mast and sail. As he looked towards the barn a sudden thwack of a sheet made him jump and quickened an impulse to escape back to the safety of the trees. He stared up at where the trees stood tall in the rising wind. What if she was there, watching him now just as he had watched her? A shiver passed through his body like the wind in the field of grass.

In front was the red barn door, wooden pallets and sacking nailed to the window frames. Purple-headed weeds sprouted from crevices along the base of the wall. He looked about him once more to check that he was alone and then tried the door but it was locked as he already knew it would be, and its solid frame resisted all of his half-hearted efforts to push it open. Moving to the windows he put his eyes to the gaps between the slats of wood and peered into the gloom. Almost at once he pulled his head back as if he had been punched, the smell unlike anything he had ever known. Living on a farm had taught him about smells, but this one was different. It was not the uncovered slurry pit, the rotting carcass of a sheep hidden in reeds by the stream, the stored mound of turnip to be used as winter feed.

He pinched his nose and looked again and that was when he heard it – the low, almost inaudible whimpering, but mixed with it was another sound, the strangled, guttural breathing of some animal he could not recognise. He pushed his face closer to a knotted gap in the slats and thought he glimpsed the shuffling shape of some shadowy creature. The noise grew louder, more insistent, and he suddenly felt that it sensed his presence, the way a dog knows when some stranger has encroached on its territory. The sounds were not fierce, but almost pleading; not falling or rising beyond the whimper but a low, steady, plaintive sob which held him with its strangeness and for which, despite his frantic searching, he could find no reference in his memory. A little louder now, maybe closer, and with it a flurry of smell, infused with some festering sore.

84

He pulled back his head to breathe clearer air and as he did so the sacking trembled behind the pallet. He wanted to turn and run, run and hide in the heart of the trees, but the creature was calling to him now, a wordless pleading, breaking on itself and now rising again in a fragmented and desperate rhythm of need. The sacking moved an inch from the wall leaving a narrow margin of darkness, and then just above the sill and from behind a tiny half-moon-shaped knot in the wooden band of pallet, he saw it moving towards him. His heart banged in his chest and he stepped back, frightened that somehow it might seek to drag him into the blackness of the barn, but it rested on the stone sill, thin, shorter than his own, ingrained with dirt, the long ragged nail speckled with white and brittle-looking like the shell of an egg. The whimpering had stopped and there was only the rustling, shuddering breathing behind the sacking which trembled now like a veil. And then he stepped forward and slid his own finger along the sill until the two tips touched.

Then he was gone, running through the long grass using his hands like a swimmer to speed his path, along the river bank, running until the hot stabbing pain in his side forced him to stop. But still he walked, both hands on his hips like handles on a jug, his breathing coming in deep retches. Stooping down, he splashed his face with water, dipping his hand into the reflection of clouds, then started to run again. And when the pain pierced his side the memory of the sounds twisting round his head spurred him on and would not let him stop.

He found his father in the lower fields cutting hedges, the lane smudged with black, thorned clippings, but his breathless story bewildered him and he had to repeat it again and again. He did not tell his father everything, but when it looked as though he would turn again to his hedge cutting, he pulled his father's arm with an urgency and a familiarity that startled them both. He knew his father did not understand, thought it was only some child who had accidentally got locked in, but he did not care if only his father would come and set him free. He clambered up behind him on the tractor and the noise of the engine prevented any further conversation, but he could sense his father's feeling of exasperation in the stiffness of his posture and the roughness of his gear changes.

His father knew without needing directions where the house was and as the tractor trundled slowly up the lane leading to it he tightened his hand on his father's broad shoulder. Impatiently, he watched him knock at the door of the house then walk towards the barn. His father kept asking him if he was sure, as if not totally convinced that he had not made up the whole thing, or that it was not part of some childish game, and for a terrible moment he began to doubt his own memory. But as they came closer to the locked door and the blocked-out windows he remembered the touch of the finger and knew that it was real.

His father tried to open the door, his large hands rattling the lock, then put his head to it and listened, both palms pressed against the wood above his head. He called out but there was only silence and when he turned round there was irritation on his face, an expression that said his suspicions had been realised. Before, it would have been a look which would have silenced him, driven him to shelter, but now he grew desperate and begged his father to listen again, showing him the gap in the wood where the finger had appeared. His father ran his hand along the sill dismissively and as he did so they both heard the soft whimper from inside. He clattered the pallets with his fists and called out again and again, asking if there was someone there but the only response was the rising whimper.

His father's face had changed now, as if finally it had come awake, and he sent him running across the yard to fetch the axe with a voice driven by urgency. He had to twist and jerk it with both hands before he freed it from the wood, and as he ran he almost tripped, his knee banging against the blunt edge of the axe-head. In his father's face he saw the uncertainty which had replaced his familiar calm self-confidence and as he took the axe he hesitated, holding it in his hands as if feeling for its balance while he tried to decide what to do.

With a sharp jerk of his hand he motioned him to one side and the axe was swinging towards the door in a great slicing arc. The noise of the cracking, splintering wood was terrible to him as if something secret, almost delicate, was being broken in front of him and he closed his eyes as the axe rose and fell again and again. As it clattered to the ground he opened his eyes to see his father holding on to the wall with one hand and kicking in the lacerated door until it flapped inwards, vibrating in the sudden surge of silence like a plucked chord.

Without moving they both stared at the fan of light which squirmed across the barn, lighting up the soiled whorls of straw, the smear of shit, the scraps and husks of food strewn across the stinking floor, felt the hot, fetid stench hit their senses. His father rubbed the back of his hand across his mouth, told him to stay where he was, then dipping his head to clear the lintel, entered the barn.

He watched his father hesitate, then step out of the fantail of light and disappear into the shadows, heard him say, 'God in heaven,' repeating it two or three times, but softer each time, and then he was talking too softly to hear the words but it sounded like the way he would speak to some frightened animal which might bolt at any second. The whimpering had grown louder again and it was accompanied now by strangled hawking noises.

His father suddenly stepped back into the light but his face was turned away and he did not speak except to tell him to stay where he was and not to move from that spot. He waited in confusion as he walked back across the yard and then realised his father was going for the sheet flapping on the line, going to wrap whatever was in the barn in it. His father walked slowly as if each step was heavy with thought and, unable any longer to resist the impulse, he edged into the barn, his hand covering his mouth and nose like a mask. He stared through the grained striations of darkness which seemed to crackle and pulse like static, and squinted into the wavering pockets of shadows. His eyes blinked and focussed again.

It was the pale frost of face he saw first, a tiny blur of white with dark hollows of eyes, shrouded by a tangled mane of matted hair which stretched to his shoulders. Hair smirched and sodden with shit. A boy, maybe five or six years old – it was hard to tell. Completely naked, the raised ridges of his ribs pushing through his skin. He was crouched on a nest of straw like a small bird and then he stood up, his skinny sticks of legs were bowed and misshapen and covered in pussed scabs like scum on the surface of stagnant water.

As his eyes grew accustomed to the gloom he saw the boy's lips were moving in wordless speech, quicker and quicker like some small fish impaled on a hook and gasping for life. He willed the words to come out but they seemed to choke and flounder into nothingness. The only sound came from the flies buzzing round his head. Struggling to subdue his own fear he stepped forward, wanting to tell him he was the boy whose finger he had touched but he, too, could not find any words, and then his father was shouting at him to get out and pushing past him with the crumpled sheet trailing across the rancid straw.

Standing in the yard he breathed in the fresh air while his father shouted to him what to do. He was to run to the Henderson place and get them to telephone for Sergeant Crosby then wait to direct the sergeant to the barn. When he had done that he was to go straight home and wait there, without speaking to anyone about what he had seen.

It seemed an eternity before the sergeant appeared, his large lumbering figure hunched over the handlebars of his heavy, black-framed bicycle, his face red with the strain and his hat pushed back on his head to let the air at his face. His corded revolver nestled snugly in its leather holster. He wanted to follow the ticking whirr of the bicycle but he had already disobeyed his father once and knew there would be trouble if he were to repeat the offence. So he set off for home as he had been ordered to do, but as he ran the fear in his stomach loosened and he was sick in a ditch, heaving until his stomach was empty. And in his imagination he saw the child animal wrapped in the folds of the sheet, the curved bones of his spindle legs dangling like bruised stalks, his hollow eyes blinking in the fierce and frightening light of the world. Heard, too, once more, the strange choking sounds rasping in the boy's throat.

*

'And you never saw him again?'

They stood in the yard where grass and weeds fought each other for space, and looked about them.

'No, just those few seconds. That was all.' He pushed his hand through his hair. His mouth felt dry and he wanted to spit. Then he told her things she knew already because the words broke the silence which pushed down on them too heavily. Told her about having to give evidence in court, of the crowd of women who waited outside the court-house to jeer at her, the stories in the papers.

'And do you know what happened to him?' He felt her hand fumble for his.

'They took him to a home somewhere. I think he had operations to straighten his legs but he never learned to speak. That's all I know.'

They stood facing the stone barn. There was no door now, or blocked-out windows, just a dark frame of shadows and on parts of the wall the plaster had flaked away, leaving slabs of rough stone exposed. He moved closer to the doorway but he could feel her reluctance in the tightness of her grip and he, too, hesitated.

'How could anyone do something like this, John? Do it to their own child,' she asked, her voice almost a whisper.

'I don't know. Maybe she was sick, maybe she was to be pitied as much as he was. I never think of her.'

'But you do think of him, don't you?' She was looking at him closely and for a second he thought of lying to her but knew he could not carry it off, and he wanted to hear his own truth, because the place in which they stood would brook no lies. He had to tell her.

'Yes, I think of him sometimes, more often since we came back here to live. And sometimes it's in my dreams. I think of him being kept here all that time without anyone knowing and what it must've been like – the darkness, always the darkness, and then the sound of the key in the lock and the door opening a splinter of light. Sometimes I think I hear that whimpering, over and over, in my head.' The words rushed out as if glad to be released.

'And what world did he live in? I think about that. Was it a human world and how could it have been when he never experienced any of the things which make us human? And if it wasn't a human world then what was it, where was it? And when he felt the touch of my finger did he know he had touched someone who was the same as him?'

He paused for breath and was conscious that for the first time in a long while he was sharing something with her which was secret and private. It was too late to stop.

'But mostly I think about what it was he tried to say, of the need which forced those terrible sounds into his throat. Standing there naked in the darkness, what did he try to say? But maybe they were only sounds which had no meaning. I don't know.'

He stared again into the open doorway but he could feel the pull of her hand and he knew he could take her no further. He put his arm around her shoulders and they turned back the way they had come. They walked slowly through the scraggy scrub of weeds and grass, picking their steps with care, their voices low and intimate, the way people speak at a funeral or in church. Ahead suddenly, a bird shot up out of the grass, its flapping crack of wings quickening the beat of their hearts.

*

He had written to the McQuarries, asking them to make an appointment, but had received no reply. A fortnight later he telephoned and spoke to Mrs McQuarrie. She was hesitant and said she would get her husband to ring him, but the call never came. He was not sure what to do. He could not have the child assessed by the educational psychologist without her parents' permission. In the meantime he arranged for her to get extra help with reading and writing. It only amounted to one half hour slot a week, but it was the best he could do.

She would look at him now when he took her class for history and when he spoke to her would answer with a few barely distinguishable words. But she seemed interested in what they were doing, and with as much individual help as he could manage, she was able to complete some of the tasks in a limited way. A couple of times he persuaded Emma to come in and work with the class. She had prepared templates and drawings of Celtic jewellery and the children made copies in air-hardened clay and then painted them. With Emma's help, Jacqueline made a Celtic cross with a tiny hole for her to thread through some string or wool.

She seemed to enjoy working with the children and spent a long time at home in preparation. Her only condition about coming was that he should keep her out of the staffroom and he was happy to oblige, shielding her particularly from Mrs Haslett's inspection. He had escaped major confrontation with Haslett only because he had not given her any opportunity, but he knew that it was probably just a matter of time before their wills crossed. He found himself wondering if it would ever be possible to really make anything of the school while she and Vance were such an established part of the place.

She had sniffed a little about his first joint history trip to the monastic site at Nendrum with Liam Hennessy's Holy Cross, but had said nothing directly and he found it difficult to gauge what she was thinking. He was a little surprised, too, when Jacqueline brought in a permission slip from her parents.

The day itself was overcast and the pre-warned children came equipped with wellingtons and rainwear. The bus had collected the children from Holy Cross first and when it arrived they had filled the back half. Hennessy was stretched over two seats smoking a pipe. They had never met before and they shook hands and exchanged comments about the weather prospects. He was slightly older than he had anticipated, with receding grey hair and a thin flush of a face which hinted at an acquaintanceship with drink. He wore an elbow-patched tweed jacket, flannels and a pair of trainers which looked as though they had been borrowed for the day. The smoke from his pipe curdled in the damp draught which seeped through the bus. The two sets of children eyed each other briefly with a mixture of curiosity and suspicion, then turned to their own friends and their own conversations.

'Did you have any objections, then?' Hennessy asked.

'No, none. And you?'

'None. Parents seemed happy enough and any that weren't are keeping it to themselves.'

A thin smattering of rain sprinkled the windows as they chatted about their schools, and when the discussion turned to the new proposals for assessment, Hennessy took his pipe out of his mouth in order to swear more freely.

'A load of absolute shite – excuse my French, but it's enough to turn anyone's head. Martin Trainor – get your feet off the back of that seat before I come down there and skelp your legs!' He gestured elaborately with his pipe.

'Listen, John, I've been in this game a brave few years now and let me tell you something for nothing. Whatever you do, do nothing, keep your head well down and there's a good chance it'll all pass overhead. One thing's certain – don't go running round like a headless chicken turning your school upside down for the goalposts'll move a right few more times before they're stuck in cement.' He nodded sagely in agreement with himself, only breaking his self-absorption to shout at another miscreant. 'In the name of God, Malachy Brogan, take those headphones off before they set on your ears and try talking to someone. It's a quaint old custom called conversation, very popular in days gone by.' (And, as an aside) 'Nowadays they call it social interaction.' He winked at him and puffed on the pipe. 'Typical bloody EMU. Put the two tribes on a bus and you're supposed to be on the way to the promised land, when one half's spitting out the windows and the other half are wired up to some bunch of heavy metallers. Still, it looks good for the inspectors and the money flows like holy water. Have you had any of the Key Stage cops out with you yet, John?'

'No, not yet, but I've a probationer, so no doubt we'll see an inspector at some stage.'

'Well, when you do, give them short shrift and they'll not be back in too big a hurry.'

Hennessy had seemed quite normal on the telephone, but he enjoyed him and found himself feeding him lines like a straight man in a comedy act.

'Have I been to the training days? If I have to sit once more and listen to some arse-bandit tell me that he doesn't know any more of the answers than I do, then I'm going to tell him to bugger off and get somebody who does! That's the trouble with this bloody shooting match – you never get to meet the boys who've their fingers on the triggers.'

The rain was falling more steadily now and he took the opportunity of a lull in his colleague's conversation to hand out the work-sheets he had made. It was a kind of trail where they had to gather information about the monastic site and then use it to work out some answers as to how the monks might have lived and worked. He wasn't sure if Hennessy was taking a hand out of him or not, but he had to supply him with a copy of the answers, and he began to wonder if he had done any of the preparation work they had planned.

Soon the bus was crossing the narrow stone bridge on to Mahee Island and slowly negotiating the twisting road which led to the site of the ruins. Now the full attention of the children was focused on the world outside, where ploughed fields sloped down to Strangford Lough and the stony shore-line where the ebbed tide had left knots of worm casts and seaweed-draped rocks. Some of them spotted swans and others clambered up the back of their seats to share in the sighting. When the bus stopped, Hennessy stood up at the front and gave out final instructions. They had already been divided into groups of four, two from each school, and he gave them their orders to work well together and a final warning about behaviour.

'Now, listen, ladies and gentlemen. There has been a mon-astic site on this place since the seventh century. Yes, Leanne, it's even older than I am, and when we all get back on this bus I expect it to have been left exactly as we found it. You don't wander off to the shore. It's on private property and is patrolled by alsatians who would savage you as soon as look at you, and you don't climb any walls or throw stones. And let me tell you one other thing. Up in the outer cashel there's a pit dug and it has a sign above it which says, "Pit of uncertain origin." That means they've never worked out what it was used for, but I'll tell you what it'll be used for today – anyone I see dropping sweetie papers or Coke tins or scratching their initials on the stones. Now, leave your lunches on the bus, but take your coats and clipboards and line up at the side of the bus. And, Malachy, unless you want to walk home, don't even think of bringing those earphones.'

While Hennessy was speaking, he watched his own pupils studying him with amazement, some with widening eyes when he mentioned the pit. The children from Holy Cross stared impassively, obviously inured to his style of delivery.

When both schools had got off the bus and formed into their groups they set off up the incline, only to come running back when they realised they needed to extract information from the site map at the boundary wall. He watched Jacqueline trailing her group at a safe distance and it jarred to think that within a few minutes the two children from the other school would discover what her fellow pupils already knew. He hoped they would be kind but it was only a slim chance. Perhaps he should not have put her into a group and instead got her to stay with him, but no matter what way he might have organised it, the end result would have been the same.

Under a grey, flat sky the children scampered up the slope towards the concentric circles of dry stone walls, whose surfaces were blotched and whitened with weathering. He hoped they would not be disappointed by what they were finding – lines of stone, like rows of blackened teeth, the skeleton of the church and the stump of the round tower. It needed imagination to construct a living image from the paucity of the remains, and that was a skill which they found increasingly difficult when everything in their world came to them complete and instantaneous. But as he watched them it was obvious that the game element of their exploration held their attention as they whirled about the site like dervishes, the wind flapping open unbuttoned coats or tweaking baseball caps from startled heads. He paused on a large, pock-marked stone and listened to his colleague below enlightening a cluster of attentive faces.

'You understand now about the Vikings. A violent lot they were – a bit like English football fans abroad you see on the telly – and everywhere they went there was blood and thunder and splitting of heads. And everything that wasn't screwed down they lifted and took back home.'

He didn't stay for the rest of the exposition but walked on again, following the curved line of the stone wall, occasionally touching stones with his hand, wondering what other hands might have touched the same place. Sometimes a group of children would run up to him, seeking help with some of their questions, and he gave the answers in the form of easy clues. The wind played with someone's dropped work-sheet and a child raced after it, stamping only grass with his foot as the wind maliciously swirled it further after a second's pause.

At the outer wall closest to the shoreline, he gathered a couple of groups round him. Jacqueline was there, her cropped blonde hair blown into a tattered bird's nest, her nose dripping, unnoticed, until it splashed on to her work-sheet and was then staunched with the sleeve of her nylon Peter Storm. He got them to look over the top of the wall and down across the lough where the wind ribbed the water and black-faced gulls flew parallel and close to its patterned surface. In the distance were the humped tree-lines of other islands, the bob of boats moored in Whiterock.

'Why do you think they might have built the site here?'

'Because you got good views of everywhere all about.'

'Yes, that's right. And why do you think views were important?'

They screwed up their faces in concentration as gulls cackled overhead.

'Sir, because you could see anybody coming and they couldn't sneak up on you.'

'Good man, Robert. Now, I want all of you to do something for me. I want you to imagine that we've got in our time machine and travelled back all those years, right back to the tenth century and this is where we live and work. And maybe it was a day just like this with a strong wind blowing and the same gulls flying about and you're standing just right here, maybe taking a rest from your work and then you look up.' He pointed far into the lough. 'And you see something, something small at first, but it's coming closer and it's got a white sail and you know from its carved prow and rows of oars that

97

it's a longship. Look hard, can you see it coming smoothly, steadily, through the white-tipped waves? Can you see it?' He had lowered his voice to a whisper as they peered into the distance, searching their imaginations for it.

'And as you stand right here watching it come closer all the time, the wind pushes out the sail towards you and you see what's on it. And what you see makes your heart jump and then beat faster and faster because on the sail is a black hawk. And a black hawk means . . .' He trailed off as if he had forgotten the meaning and as he did so a chorus of steaming voices shouted, 'The Vikings! The Vikings!'

'You're right, it's the Vikings!' he shouted back, simulating panic. 'And in not very long they'll be ashore, what'll we do? What'll we do?'

'Run!' shouted Lisa.

'Wet yourself,' offered an anonymous voice from the huddle.

'And after you've wet yourself, what'll you do? Hurry, hurry, every second's precious!' He bounced back and forwards from the wall, counterfeiting a rising and infectious panic.

'Sir, run away and hide.'

'But what about everyone else, what about all your friends?'

'Warn them by shouting.'

'But maybe they're working away over there and your voice can't carry in the wind.'

'Ring the bell!'

'Good, Tony, ring the bell. Take Gerard and go quickly to the tower and ring it. Loudly, now, so everyone can hear.'

The two boys looked at each other then sprinted off to the tower and set up a boisterous ding-dong.

'And the rest of you, are you just going to run away and let the Vikings take all the most valuable possessions of the monastery?'

A few thought yes, but more shouted no.

'Well, then, quickly, we've only a few minutes left – what'll we take? Think hard, think hard. Remember what we did in class.'

'The books and Bibles with the drawings!'

'Good, quickly, take someone to the church and get them.'

'The golden chalice!'

'Right, quickly, go and get it, Lucy. There's not much time.'

'The animals!'

'Yes, we can't leave them behind. You both go and round them up. Think hard about where they'll be.'

The group had almost dissolved. The two remaining boys had drawn twig swords, held a practice duel and were now preparing to repel the invaders. Only Jacqueline stood unoccupied. His mind had run out of tasks and as he struggled to create one for her he saw that her eyes were watering in the wind and then he realised she was crying. He led her aside, angling her into the privacy of the stone wall and crouched down on his haunches.

'What's the matter, Jacqueline?'

She shook her head slowly from side to side, the tears welling up in her eyes, and with her finger touched a whorl of moss on the face of one of the stones.

'Did your group go off and leave you?'

She shook her head again and he knew it was not the reason. Soon, the other children would be returning with their gathered treasure trove.

'Tell me what's the matter. Please, Jacqueline.'

She stared at the ground and her whispered answer was almost lost in the rising wind. 'The Vikings are coming.'

He fumbled in his pocket for a handkerchief and, putting his arm around her, dried her face. 'It was only a game, it wasn't real, Jacqueline. It was only a pretend game. The Vikings aren't really coming.'

Part of him wanted to laugh, part of him was ashamed at having scared her. It was starting to rain and he directed all the returning children back to the bus. They charged down the slope, shrieking and screeching like the circling gulls. He could see Hennessy hunched in the ruin of the church, trying to re-light his pipe. Taking her hand – it felt cold and very small – he led her back the long way, walking slightly in front to shelter her from the wind.

*

Listening to her describe it, it sounded like an SAS operation, complete with smoke flares, tape measurements, stopwatch timings. But at the end of the day Mr Beattie from the Water and Sewage Department had failed to come up with any real answers to the smell. The smoke bombs released in the outside manholes had fizzled out without permeating the house and for all his sniffing and pacing around, he had been unable to locate the origin of the problem. It was predictable too, of course, that the day he chose to arrive there was no trace of the smell, almost as if it was hiding from detection. He had checked the septic tank and studied the time it took for flushed paper to reach it, but the best he could do was to arrange for the tank to be emptied and promise that he would return with a colleague if the smell should appear in the next few weeks.

Emma was increasingly exasperated by the problem and increasingly irrational in her demands that it should be fixed, almost as if she felt he should be able to conjure up some magic spell to make it disappear. Neither of them could think of anything more that could be done but it did not stop her pushing the burden of finding a solution on to him. Once he found himself about to remind her that she had been the one determined to buy an older property, oblivious to the potential problems such a purchase could bring. While the new carpets had gone some way to taking the coldness out of the house, it was obvious, although not expressed, that the place was too big for them. There were too many rooms, too many spaces which remained unfilled and each one reminded of the absence of family. Her parents had given them several older pieces of furniture which fitted the style of the house but did little to lessen the gap between reality and the pictures in magazines.

Early morning incursions by rabbits had already consumed some of the shrubs she had planted in the garden and the exorbitant quotes they had received from landscapers had postponed any plans she had harboured. The one positive thing was, she had started painting again, often working from photographs she had taken. Sometimes she left him off at school then drove into the Mournes and spent the day sketching and photographing. Mostly, she painted water-colours, occasionally selling one in a gallery or to one of her parents' circle. They were generally local landscapes and if he was really honest he did not much care for them. They were delicate and pretty, but somehow vague and undefined – pale washes of gentle colour which filtered all the grit and rawness out of the landscape. It was easy to see them as a reflection of her personality and he was increasingly aware, more than ever before, of those aspects of her which left him with a feeling of disappointment.

He was old enough to understand that in a relationship there was always shift and resettlement, that weaknesses and irritations were invariably counterbalanced by other virtues, but in the last year he was conscious that his thinking about her had started to change. He felt more and more that he was caring for her and loving her in a way that was not dissimilar to the way he cared for the children in his trust. And if anything, he felt he was getting less back from her than them, but he knew, too, it was a difficult time for her, and he consoled himself with the belief that soon things might fall back into place, revert to what they had been before.

The painting was a good sign. She had got her studio looking well and if she could sell a painting or two it would lift her spirits. Maybe if he had a quiet word with her father he might pull a string or two. And although on occasions his own mood could swing dramatically, he tried to tell himself that school was going quite well. No one could expect sweeping changes in a couple of months but in his own mind he was able to catalogue his successes. He had got a Parent-Teacher Association off the ground, set up working parties to facilitate the development of the new curriculum, had an EMU scheme up and running. Eric had even put up the new notice-boards in the foyer. On the negative side, he had to admit that the spirit of Reynolds still lingered like a thin layer of dust over the school and, despite his own ideals and approaches, it was certain that staff like Vance and Haslett continued to teach in the way they always had. That would prove a long-term struggle and one about which he had no great expectation of success.

There was, too, an exceptional closure day approaching for schools to work on their new curriculum and plan approaches to assessment, but despite his best efforts he had been unable to find anyone in the Area Board prepared to put their head on the line and lead the session. He would have to do it himself and he knew it was a potential minefield through which he would be lucky to find a safe path. And Mrs Craig still had a leaking roof.

As he sat in his study thinking of the best strategy he could hear Emma pottering about in the kitchen. He glanced at the two unpacked tea-chests which sat in the corner of the room.

They were filled with books and records for which he had not yet organised shelving. He started to browse through them, lifting and examining mementoes of the past – the books and ideas a young man thought were important, the values on which you thought you could build a world. *On the Road*, his copy of *Blonde on Blonde*, *Astral Weeks*. Hendrix and Leonard Cohen LPs, more books and records a street map of Amsterdam. They all seemed embarrassingly dated, curios from another age, objects of potential derision. With a smile he thought that if the eight good men who had appointed him had been able to view the subversive contents of these chests he would never have got his job. But it all seemed so distant and harmless, even naïve – one more generation's striking of a pose. His eye caught the grey cover of *The Catcher in the Rye*. He had not read it in ten years. He was flicking the pages when Emma came in. Phoebe – he had really liked that name, had even suggested they use it if it was a girl, but Emma had laughed at him and dismissed it from her list of possibilities.

'A stroll down memory lane?'

'Yeh, I'll have to get shelves organised.'

She lifted a Hendrix LP and stared at the cover. 'You must have been a bit of a hippy.'

'Long hair, flares, paisley shirts – the lot. But everyone had long hair in those days and don't pretend you don't remember.'

'You're forgetting, Mr Cameron, I was a child of the Seventies, not the Sixties. Abba, The Bay City Rollers, platform shoes. You made me read that book though, made me feel I wasn't a complete human being because I'd missed out on it. Always the teacher, always trying to complete my education.'

'Well, here's a question for you, Miss Cameron. Why is it called *The Catcher in the Rye*?'

While she screwed up her face in pretend thought and made her eyes cross, he flicked through more pages.

'It was something about Holden Caulfield and wanting to catch all the children before they fell over some cliff. I can't remember exactly and anyway, I only pretended to like the book, like I pretended to like all those other books you made me read and the records you made me listen to. After you'd gone home I'd put on my Abba records, "Dancing Queen" and Elton John and skim a few pages so I could pretend I'd read them.'

They both laughed and she sang a few bars of 'Dancing Queen', moving round herself in a little parody of a dance.

'It was Holden's dream where all these thousands of kids are playing in a big field at the edge of some huge cliff and if any of them were running or not looking where they were going, close to the edge, he'd catch them. He'd be the catcher in the rye – that's all he wanted to be.'

She stopped dancing and draped her arm across his shoulders. 'And that's how John Cameron sees himself – as the catcher in the rye?'

He felt himself blushing, laughing off her suggestion. 'Don't be stupid, you've been listening to too much junk music. You're brain damaged. And there aren't any cliffs around here for anyone to fall over.'

She ruffled his hair and smiled at his embarrassment then went back into the kitchen to make his packed lunch for the morning. He could still hear her humming and he resisted the temptation to play some of his records on the stereo, knowing that no other music could sound so welcome. He threw the book back into the tea-chest. Perhaps he kept too many things from the past, too many objects which should have been jettisoned. But he found it hard to discard the pieces which fitted together to form the pattern of his memory.

She was getting ready for bed as he locked up the house. Each night she simply announced her departure and left him to turn off lights and television and lock doors and windows. He should have spent some more time planning the in-service training day, but he could not face it and joined her in the bedroom.

She was reading a magazine and he could see sweeping herbaceous borders, harmonious chromatic progressions. Although he read for a short while his mind was not really on it and when she set her magazine aside he followed suit. As the light went out he snuggled up behind her, his arm protectively round her waist. She was singing gently to herself, like a child lulling herself to sleep, and then she stopped and moved his hand from her waist and placed it on her breast. He cupped it lightly in his hand and kissed the swathe of freckles which ran across her shoulder blades and as he did so he felt her nipple harden. Turning round, she kissed him and held him tightly, then slipped her body under his. He hesitated, and though everything in her body told him it was all right, he was suddenly frightened of hurting her and his fear made him clumsy and she had to help him. Slowly, gently, like it was the first time, and then instinct took over and he was talking to her and kissing her and calling her stupid names like his dancing queen and everything was just like it had been before. But as he gave himself up to the rhythm of his desire, tried to fill the emptiness of his need, it was another voice he heard − the pleading, whimpering voice of his dreams. And across his mind like some frightened bird flapped a jagged series of images which he could not control or stop − Jacqueline's face dropping like a stone on to her book, the gulls falling like snow into the open field, their circling cries above Nendrum. Tumbling after one another in a welter of tangled confusion which swept through him and which he could not control. And through them all the distant, plaintive cry of a child and then, in a crystallisation of fear, he knew that what he heard in his dreams was their own child, lost and drifting in some veiled and shuttered world from which he could never escape. Calling to him as he faded back into the gathering shadows.

She had stopped moving and was looking up at him in confusion. He gave himself back to the rhythm but despite his frantic efforts to focus his mind, re-find his passion, he knew that it was gone. He faked a sheepish smile and apologised, then rolled on to his back.

'What happened?'

'I just lost it. Maybe I was nervous or something.'

'It's been a long time – you're out of practice.'

'Emma, you'll not be buying me one, then.'

'Buying you what?'

'One of those mugs that says "world's greatest lover".'

She nestled into his side and in a few minutes was asleep. He lay awake, his arm under her head until it grew numb, and then he gently eased it free.

He didn't turn on the attic light but paused at the top of the short flight of stairs until his eyes had grown accustomed to the soft sheen of light which seeped in from the moon. The wooden floorboards were cold and smooth under his feet as he picked his way carefully through the discarded sprawl. In his rational mind he felt the incredible foolishness of the thought that now lodged there like some spore. He was neither superstitious nor religious by nature, and clung to no belief in any world other than the one he could see and touch, but the more he tried to brush the image away, the more it seemed to burst and spread through his being.

He sat on an old cane rocking chair Emma had paid too much money for in a jumble sale and stored for the day when she would repair it. Then he moved aside the two screening tea-chests and lifted the suitcase on to his knees. He felt his mind existed in some limbo world between sleep and waking. A white-winged moth trembled against the glass of the sky-light. Sifting through the contents of the case, he held each object carefully before returning it to its original place. He forced himself to think of the most solid, concrete objects which existed – the document on assessment, the postcard from Reynolds, the brackish pools of water on the railway line. Anything which anchored his mind to the tangible world and blocked out the thought that had so shaken him.

At the bottom of the case he found a copy of the four-month scan. He stared at the monochrome print – fuzzy like some sonar under-water image – but the foetal shape was still recognisable. He had been a good father, had read all the books, knew that at that moment of development fingers and toes and their nails had formed and eyebrows and eyelashes were beginning to grow. It was a strange consolation now to tell himself that the embryo had been carried away in a metal dish, bagged and incinerated. Whatever life had been created through the mystery of conception had ended in that moment. There was no lost child, no wandering, frightened waif calling for his father. There was no other world than this and the only thing which had spawned this misery was his physical and mental tiredness, the stress of a new job. He sat back in the silvery light and surveyed the clutter which swelled all around him and tried to spark some warming memory from a familiar object. When he felt his calm returning he shut the case and returned it to its place of concealment. Quietly he started to descend the steepness of the stairs, holding lightly on to the wooden rail but halfway down stopped, then retraced his steps. He stood on the cane chair and forced the skylight open, feeling the coolness of the air hit his face as the moth fluttered into the dark pathways of the night.

*

They formed an orderly but impatient queue to receive their gear from the store and then filed back outside, struggling not to drop anything. Equipped with their wet suits, hiking boots, buoyancy aids, orange waterproofs and safety helmets they balanced the piles precariously under their chins and lumbered off to the changing rooms. He followed the boys while Mrs Craig accompanied the girls. Hennessy had ensconced himself in the staff canteen and was enjoying coffee and a doughnut. He had been supposed to bring another member of staff but failed to produce one and gave no coherent explanation.

The boys squeezed themselves into the one-piece rubber wet suits with varying degrees of success. Some, suddenly finding themselves with dried and stiff outer skins, did impersonations of penguins, while others stood motionless like sticks of liquorice. He gave help where it was needed, making adjustments to trouser lengths and helmet straps and generally chivvied them on. Some were excited, engaging in competitive bravado, while others masked their nervousness with meticulous checking of laces and zips. They plied him with constant questions. How deep would the water be? Could you drown in the rock pools? Could you keep your watch on if it was waterproof? Then, when most of them were almost ready, he went to collect his own gear, pausing to look into the canteen to ask if Hennessy had got his canoeing equipment from the store.

'My God, John, you don't seriously think that I'm going to do a Hiawatha impersonation and get into one of those canoes? I'll be doing my supervision from the shore.' Taking another sip from his coffee, he winked at him. 'Remember the dignity of the office John, now, and don't be letting the side down, traipsing around like Jacques Cousteau.'

He smiled and left him lighting up his pipe. Hennessy's apathy couldn't diminish his own excitement. The outdoor pursuits centre had split their day into two activities – bouldering and canoeing. The two schools had been mixed and divided into two groups with a roughly equal mix of boys and girls in each. He was accompanying the group which was spending the morning bouldering, while Mrs Craig was going with the canoeing party. The centre provided experienced instructors and it was a nice break to stand back and watch someone else do all the work. As the instructor played lightly on the dangerous aspect and the need to follow instructions carefully, they listened to him intently, their faces almost unrecognisable under the helmets plumped like bowls on their heads.

A mini-bus drove them the short distance along the coast and they scampered down the path to the sea where one of the many rivers flowed down from the Mournes. Their first activity involved lying on their backs in a narrow little gully, folding their arms across their chests and simply letting the water carry them down into the pool below. Standing in the rock pool at the bottom of the chute the instructor shepherded each child across to dry land. The more adventurous of the children clamoured to go first, pushing with their heels to kick-start their momentum, while others hung back, needing more encouragement. Jacqueline was in this latter group and she and two other girls were obviously nervous about it all, but the instructor coaxed them gently until each one had completed the task and splashed into the rock pool with a mixture of relief and pride.

He felt a little nervous himself as he lay on his back in the narrow fissure and for a few seconds wondered if Hennessy hadn't been right after all. Water and swimming weren't his strong points and he was suddenly aware of the opportunities the morning presented for making a fool of himself in front of his own pupils. The gully felt too narrow for him and he remembered the instructor's warning to keep elbows well tucked in. He felt like a corpse in a coffin and as he looked up at the sky he could hear the encouraging cries of the children. At first he felt as if he was stuck, but then he arched his back and levered his body forward with his heels until the water was shooting him forward like a torpedo in a tube. Then, with a splash and an involuntary cry of shock, he was briefly immersed in coldness before bobbing and spluttering to the surface. He swam a few metres to the rocks on the other side and as he pulled himself out children slapped his back in congratulations. Water ran out of him like a tap but there was no time to feel sorry for himself as the group set off walking up the river, short legs stretching and hopping from boulder to boulder while he brought up the rear, encouraging stragglers and wondering what new challenge was waiting for them.

The stream was replenished by recent rain and the water gushed about them with white flurries cascading over rocks in a throaty sluice of sound. They walked in Indian file, each child stepping on the stones selected by the person in front, a caravanserai of orange waterproofs and blue helmets. His boots were hurting him – he'd had to take a size smaller than he usually wore – and for a brief moment he almost wished that Vance had taken up his invitation instead of declining it with something that almost approached a joke. Out of mischief he'd offered Mrs Haslett the opportunity to come, knowing how well she enjoyed playing the role of someone who faced a challenge fearlessly, then enjoyed watching her squirm her way out of it. Mrs Craig had been enthusiastic and jumped at the opportunity. She had a relaxed, capable manner with children which he admired and led him to wonder if there were a way he might get her to teach further up the school. But for the moment at least, he turned his full concentration to surviving his next confrontation with stone and water. The instructor made it look easy, clinging to the handholds across a face of rock with practised ease and making the sideways crab-like movements with a minimum of strain. When he had completed it he turned to give final instructions and to warn, 'If you're going to fall, just let go. Don't try to hold on, just fall back into the water.'

It proved more difficult than it looked and the first half-dozen children fell backwards into the water to a malicious cheer from the spectators. The footholds and crevices were not obvious and as he stood awaiting his turn he regretted not paying closer attention. The instructor squatting on the rock overhead talked the next few children through the crossing and after they completed it without slipping, they too turned to encourage the others across. The rock's surface became more slippery now as it was splashed with more water and the dampness of the clothing which had passed over it.

Soon it was Jacqueline's turn but he could see the hesitancy in her movements as she got closer to the narrow ridge which was the starting point. It pleased him to hear the other girls shouting encouragement but she was crouching lower and lower as she glanced down at the water and he could tell that she wasn't going to attempt it. As she squatted on a rock and looked towards him he told her it was all right and, in a desire to divert attention from her failure, stepped on to the ridge. It felt impossibly narrow under his feet, more like a slight seam than any kind of ledge. He clung to the face, his hands feeling the smoothness of stone for a grip, and then from the group cheering him came the chant, 'Fall in! Fall in!' He suspected the instructor was leading it and in his momentary distraction he was over-stretching, his hand was holding nothing but lichen and he was falling backwards into space. The feeling was curiously pleasant until he smacked the water, felt it rush into his ears and the mouth which he had foolishly left open.

He threatened them all with double homework for a year but as the group set off again upstream Jacqueline's head was down and she trudged through water rather than stretch to stones. He tried to raise her spirits by making a joke of his own failure but she did not respond as they engaged in a further sequence of activities and instead crouched like a mollusc on the rocks, watching but not participating, hugging a shiver of misery. He let her be – there were other children who needed his attention. He couldn't give himself exclusively to her. They reached the final activity before lunch and it was the simplest but the most intimidating – clambering a great egg-shaped rock and then jumping off into the deep pool some few metres below. From a distance it didn't seem a particularly great height but when standing on the rock itself with the noise of the white-tipped water tumbling into the pool from upstream, the black sharpness of the rocks on either side gave it a feeling of danger which only the most confident children were able to overcome. The instructor left it entirely without persuasion to the children themselves and only a handful attempted it. Despite his own fears there was no escape for him and the group urged him to the top of the rock. He stood looking over what had suddenly taken on the characteristics of a precipice above a maelstrom of angry water, and he felt distinctly uneasy. He didn't like heights and despite the chorused urging from the children couldn't bring himself to jump. He tried to talk himself into it, knew he would regret it later if he didn't complete it, but each time he drew closer to the edge something stronger pulled him back. He listened to himself make a joke about his age, then waved the white flag, and as they gathered up the group in readiness for the trek back to the bus he was aware of the little ripple of disappointment in him.

'Sir, Sir, look!'

They all turned round to stare at Jacqueline standing on top of the rock. Some of the poppers had opened on her coat and the bottom of it flapped open like the folded corner of a page. She wasn't looking at them but staring down into the water as if looking into a mirror, held motionless by her own reflection. One of the boys beside him started to shout something but he stopped him and they stood silently looking up at her. The instructor started to move back on to the rocks but he clutched the sleeve of his jacket and pulled him back. She was shuffling forward to the edge, taking tiny stiff steps like some automaton. His mouth could taste again his own fear as he had stood there and he was frightened for her, but something else made him hold on to the instructor's coat. She was right at the edge now and in the silence they could hear the pitch and plunge of the rushing water as it spilled over the rocks and lathered into the pool. And then she was jumping, her orange coat opening like wings on an insect as she disappeared below the surface of the water before bobbing up again like a blue topped cork. Now everyone was rushing to the pool's edge and the instructor was wading through the water and pulling her out like a minnow on the end of a line. Kids were patting her on the back as water dripped out of her and she was shivering a little, but her face betrayed no emotion or elation, and as they made their way down the narrow path she trailed a rivulet of water in her wake.

Hennessy was already finishing a bowl of stew when they

arrived back at the centre. Mrs Craig and the rest of the children sat in the canteen eating their packed lunches but he had obviously inveigled a hot meal from the kitchen. He had a shower and joined them. The canoeing had gone well with plenty of games and capsizing to keep everyone entertained. The children were obviously having a good time and already friendships were being formed between children in the two schools.

'Well, we got a good day for it,' Hennessy said as he took his first puff from his pipe. 'This girl here's an Olympian rower!'

'Get away with you, Liam – you must've missed me falling out of the canoe.'

'Aye, well, it was nippy enough standing about so I took a bit of a stroll round the lake to get the blood circulating.'

It struck him that Hennessy's walk had probably led directly to the canteen and the morning paper but it didn't really matter when the instructors were so experienced and in such tight control of the situation. Still puffing his pipe, he excused himself and went off to find one of his pupils who still owed the money for the trip.

'He's a bit of a character, Fiona.'

'He certainly is, but I don't think there's any harm in him, though I have to say the wink he keeps giving me suggests he'd be open for another form of mutual understanding.'

'I wouldn't worry yourself too much – I think Liam's just a bit of a talker. You wink back and he'll probably run a mile.'

They both laughed and chatted about how the different children were getting on and he told her about Jacqueline's jump and described his own failure. Then she took one more sip of her coffee and left for a moment to hurry the girls in the changing room. A morning spent in mountain water and the hot shower he'd just enjoyed had left him feeling clean and relaxed. It seemed a pity to have to spoil it by getting changed again and then mess about in some canoe which would probably be too small for his legs and he decided to take a leaf out of Hennessy's book and supervise from the shore. Anyway, he'd brought a camera with him and it would be a good chance to take some photographs. He was loading a new film when she returned and sat down again.

'Girls all right?' he asked, threading the film.

'They're fine, each regaling the other with tales of daring and disaster. True to form of course, Kelly Truesdale has lost her towel. Jacqueline's jump is also getting a fair old re-telling and the height is growing by the minute.' She sipped her coffee and looked across at him. 'Did she bang her arm this morning?'

He stopped working with the camera and looked up. 'No, I don't think so, has she hurt it?'

'She hasn't said anything but she's a lot of bruising on her upper arm. I noticed it when she was getting changed.'

'Kids get bruises, Fiona.'

'I know that – it just caught my eye. Thinking about it now though, it hasn't been done today.'

'Did you ask her about it?'

'I didn't get much sense out of her. I think she said something about falling off a gate. I don't think she wanted to talk about it.'

'Do you think I should look at it, ask her about it?'

'I don't know, I suppose it'd do no harm. She's still in her swimsuit. If you wait outside the changing rooms I'll send her out with a message – a safety helmet or something.'

They crossed the path to the changing facilities where the group going bouldering were already queuing up to get into the mini-bus. A few seconds later Jacqueline came out in her swimsuit and bare feet. She was wearing the Celtic cross round her neck. She handed him a blue helmet without speaking or looking into his face then turned away. He called after her.

'Jacqueline, that was a very brave jump this morning – I couldn't do it.'

A yellow and blue flecked patina curled like a bracelet round her upper arm.

'My goodness that's a right bruise you have on your arm. How did you get it?'

She fingered the cross around her neck and placed one of her feet on top of the other. He smoothed flat a strand of her hair. 'I fell off a gate.'

He wished she would look him in the eye.

'A gate on the farm at home?'

She nodded her head and then before he could think of what to say she turned away again and re-entered the changing rooms. He stood for a second, staring at the wet prints of her feet.

*

It was the wife of the local doctor on the phone. He had been warned about her but this was his first encounter. It wasn't going well. She was querying the value of a day spent in outdoor pursuits at a time when she felt preparing for the transfer tests would have been the priority. Despite his best efforts to reassure her she persisted in her entrenched position and it was soon apparent that she had conferred with Vance – it was even possible that he had put her up to the call as she spoke of the good job he did within the existing constraints on his time and how she was sure the fewer interruptions he had, the better the results would be in June. He let her ramble on as gradually he gave up any hope of a rational discussion. Outside his window he could see the trees smouldering into autumn colour. Eventually she ran out of steam and he thanked her for her call and said how useful it was to get feedback from parents, and then in a moment of impulsive malice, said that if she was so concerned her son would be excused any future school outings and could stay in school to receive personal attention from Mr Vance. As she struggled for a reply he excused himself to deal with an imaginary emergency and put the receiver down.

He opened the mail, scanned three or four circulars from the Department then filed them in the bin. He went down to the office where Mrs Patterson was running off the half-term news-sheet he was sending home. It was an idea new to the school and he'd included some children's descriptions of their outdoor pursuits day. In the foyer he paused and looked at the bare notice-boards which stretched round the walls. They made him nervous – they could so easily turn out to be a permanent and inescapable monument to a failed idea. He decided that if the worst came to the worst he would beg or bribe Emma to paint murals on them, but he wasn't quite prepared to concede defeat so quickly, and getting a felt-tip pen from the office and some paper, he made an arbitrary division of space and pinned up the respective class names at intervals. At least now if they remained blank the responsibility would be clearly allocated. Mrs Patterson read his thoughts and smiled.

'I don't think you need worry. By the amount of coloured paper and glue I've dispatched from this office there must be something going on. It was very devious of you because no one wants to get shown up by anyone else – a bit like going to church and everyone wanting to have the best rig-out on display.'

He pleaded a wide-eyed innocence but hoped she was right.

It turned into a day for parental complaints. He took another phone call from a mother who claimed her daughter was being teased by two other girls about her appearance, a call from a father who wondered if Miss Fulton was setting enough homework and at the end of school a Mr Watson arrived carrying a copy of *The Ghost of Johnny Franklin*, a class reader used by Mrs Haslett. It was obvious that he considered that he had come to school on a matter of urgency, explaining that he had been compelled to close his funeral parlour early and switch on his answering machine. It seemed there was no time to lose in his desire to confront the Satanic threat the book represented to any child who read it. His daughter had brought it home, he had discovered it by accident and been horrified by what he had read. He had brought a little bit of paper and he displayed the page references where offending words occurred, reading them in a rising tone: – 'poltergeist, spirits, exorcism' – building up to a crescendo in a manner which suggested he was presenting a damning indictment in a court room. When he had finished he launched into a homily on the damages to young minds from the occult, citing lurid and improbable examples of demonic possession.

He didn't know the book but even a cursory glance through it told him that it was nothing more malevolent than a children's ghost story and the possibilites of it leading to devil worship and ritual sacrifice seemed extremely remote. However, he resisted the urge to be facetious, realising only too clearly that for the man opposite it was a matter of considerable importance. He made some calculating, conciliatory remarks about how many potentially negative influences were affecting children's development, using examples of videos and anything else which came into his head and when Mr Watson was nodding he suggested that as he hadn't read the book himself he was not in the best position to pronounce judgement on it, but promised he would give it his full and early attention.

The man remained unpacified and asked to speak to Mrs Haslett. As a rule he would have insisted on acting on his staff's behalf in such a matter but he thought it probable that she would have read the book and thus been able to give a more effective response than he had constructed. He excused himself and went to her room where she was rummaging in the depths of her handbag. Before he had time to explain his visit she snapped at him about the notice-boards.

'Mr Cameron, I don't feel it's a very fair distribution of the available space when junior classes get as much space as senior ones. One of my children is surely going to produce more display work than a child at the bottom end of the school. I don't see how I can get all their work on and they've all worked very hard at it. I wouldn't want to disappoint any of them.'

Her sensitive concern for her pupils was most touching except for the fact that he knew her complaint was motivated by her persistent and petty fixation with the gradations and demarcations of status. On a better day he would have judged it a trivial enough issue over which to find some placatory compromise, but on this particular one he felt he had encountered one more miserably narrow perspective on life than he felt able to take.

'We'll have to discuss this at another time, Muriel, because at the moment I have the parent of a girl in your class in my office who thinks you're trying to recruit his daughter into the legions of Satan, through one of the books you use.'

Her mouth slipped open and she dropped her car keys back into the black hole of her bag.

'I've a meeting now with Miss Fulton, I wonder if you

119

could speak to Mr Watson, try to assure him that wasn't your intention. I assume it wasn't?'

He turned away briskly before she had a chance to formulate a reply and everything inside him was skipping. When he was in the corridor he did a little soft-shoe shuffle. Two girls coming round the corner caught him in mid-movement and simultaneously contorted their faces to suppress the rising giggles. Slipping on his stern face, he stared at them as they approached, daring them to laugh but then as they drew level he started to sing the words of 'Ghostbusters'.

He was still smiling when he opened Miss Fulton's door. She was tidying away books and paper. He had grown used to how young she looked but now he noticed how tired and pale she was. She seemed down, subdued in her movements and obviously in need of her mid-term break. He asked her if she was old enough to remember Abba but it elicited only a neutral response.

Suddenly he felt a little guilty, aware that he hadn't been able to give her the degree of support which he had hoped. His own induction to a new job had required more of his concentration than he had anticipated and there hadn't been a great deal of time left for anyone else. He tried to cheer her up by telling her of the interview going on in his office and she smiled for the first time, but when he gently mentioned the phone call about homework she started to cry, slowly at first, then more openly, searching in the top drawer of her desk for tissues. She turned her head away in embarrassment.

'I'm sorry,' she said. 'I feel rather foolish.'

'Don't worry about it,' he heard himself saying, 'everything will be all right – the first term's always the worst.' But it sounded bland and ineffectual. What he wanted to do was put his arm round her until she was cried out, but as she gradually staunched the tears he restricted himself to patting her on the back.

'You must think you've got a right cry-baby on your hands,' she said, pushing a strand of hair behind her ear.

He smiled gently but said nothing more until she was composed enough to talk.

It came scurrying out in a breathless rush, fuelled by a lack of self-confidence – the widening gap between her aspirations for her class and the daily reality, the inadequacy of her college training, a negative comment she had overheard between Vance and Haslett about her classroom control, a problem she was having with a boy in the class. He let it all come out, disappointed with himself that he hadn't detected any indications of her unhappiness earlier in the term. Then when she'd finished he tried to address the most important of the problems – her lack of self-belief – assuring her that she had made a good start in a very difficult job, repeating some of the favourable comments he'd heard and when he couldn't think of any more he made up some. He told her about some of the monumental mistakes he had made as a new teacher – the science experiment which set his desk on fire, the army of tadpoles which had swollen into frogs and invaded the whole school, the day he had taken a class to the Ulster Museum and left a child behind.

She looked as if she wasn't sure if he was making them up or not but it didn't matter because she had left her tears firmly behind. They spent some time discussing the problems in detail, working out a range of options and positive approaches, and he promised her that he would give her more active support than he had previously managed. He tried to make her feel the potential of her value to the school, the contribution she could make, and without mentioning names he let her know that he needed her support in the struggle against what he laughingly described as 'the forces of darkness'.

She had brightened to her normal self and was grateful to him for his help but he dismissed his contribution.

'Some day soon I'll probably need you to do the same for me,' he said, 'everybody gets down sometimes.' As she started to pack up her things he glanced round her room. 'You didn't manage to produce any display work for the entrance?'

'Yes, it's over there on the back table, all ready – I just didn't want to be the first to put it up.'

'You'd be doing me a big favour if you'd lead the way – I wake up in the middle of the night with nightmares about bare boards.'

She laughed and promised that she would.

In the morning after assembly she had her class in the foyer and in a short while her display space was covered with a mosaic of autumnal leaves, both real and paper, along with poems the children had written on leaf-shaped pages. Pictures of squirrels peeped out from the camouflage of leaves edged with crimson and the garland of hips, berries and acorns which formed a framework. By lunch-time, three other displays had appeared and by the end of the school everyone's was there, including Haslett's and Vance's. Most of the other classes had gone for firework displays and the foyer was a sudden frieze of colour where rockets made out of coloured paper and cardboard tubes from toilet rolls zoomed across black, sugar-paper skies awash with glitter. Wooden Catherine wheels whirled luminous fantails of sparks and Roman Candles erupted like Vesuvius in cascades of tinfoil and fluorescence.

He stood in the middle of the incandescence and when he was sure no one was watching, stretched out his arms like the wings of a plane and spun himself in a slow circle. It didn't matter that Mrs Haslett's display looked like someone had thrown a plate of pasta against the wall, it didn't matter if Vance's rockets only followed perfectly vertical and parallel trajectories. What he saw was infinitely beautiful to him and he re-lived that feeling he'd had on the first morning when he'd stood on the stage and watched the sunlight wash over the upturned faces.

'It looks well,' Mrs Patterson said, coming out of her office.

He could have kissed her but confined himself to a smile that felt as though it stretched from ear to ear and nodded his head in silent agreement. Only Eric's appearance from his dark hole of a store splashed cold water on the moment. He stared at the displays with a look of confusion, as if assessing some abstract work of art of which he did not quite see the point.

'The heating's going to dry out those leaves, Mr Cameron, and those berries and things, and then they'll fall off and get tramped into the floor.'

'Look at those fireworks, Eric!' He wanted one of them to ignite his soul, even for one fleeting moment.

'Sure isn't it a Pagan festival just like Christmas,' he replied, pushing his brush and his misery further down the corridor.

Two children appeared with a message for the office and he asked them both to point out their work and talk about how they had constructed their fireworks. It suddenly struck him that it would have been a good idea to have organised a Hallowe'en disco and firework display. Perhaps the P.T.A. might have got involved but when he reflected on it he supposed the cost would have been prohibitive. He was feeling the way he did when he was happy, fizzling away inside like one of the fireworks on display and wanting everyone to feel the same way. Three days' holiday coming up if only he could clear the hurdle of the in-service day. It would be a day bristling with danger and he knew if he didn't handle it well it could all end in disaster. As his euphoria started to ebb he took one last look at the displays then set off to photocopy some of the material he intended to use.

*

As a kind of softener, an attempt to set people off in the right mood he had scheduled the start of the day's programme for 9.30 a.m. He dressed casually as did most of the rest of the staff. Only Vance wore his school uniform of suit, white shirt, graduate tie. When they had gathered in the staffroom he began by thanking them for the excellence of their displays, hoping that Mrs Haslett wouldn't resurrect the matter of space, and quickly went on to outline the schedule for the day. He had tried to set precise times for the different sessions, attempting to ensure that things wouldn't either get bogged down or ramble into inconsequence. The morning would cover the new programmes of study in Maths and Science and in the afternoon he would attempt to grasp the nettle of assessment.

He tried to begin with an air of confidence. 'When I was preparing for today, wondering exactly where to start, I came across a Chinese proverb. It says, "Chaos equals opportunity", and the more I thought about it, the more I thought it was the key to finding a positive attitude to what's going on in education today.' He looked round the ring of faces, eager to enlist any evidence of support.

'What we need to find is some sensible path through the welter of changes which have been legislated, keep the best of what we already have, and gradually absorb the best of the new ideas.'

He reflected on the difficulties which change brought and the need for all organisations and individuals to constantly engage in self-assessment and seek to evolve. But he could tell by some of the faces that change was a word filled with fear and suspicion. For some, too, he suspected that it represented an impossibility – they had evolved to the limit of their ability and couldn't psychologically or physically cope with any more.

Mrs Douglas led off with a discussion paper on the proposals for science and she was well prepared and efficient in her delivery of the changes they would be required to introduce. When she finished there was a discussion on the implications for curriculum time and resources. Haslett made a disparaging comment about the standard of training and soon everyone was chipping in. Then Mrs Craig read out an example of a suggested experiment involving the counting of insects and there was a frenzy of criticism which he made no attempt to deflect. There were too many attainment targets, too many problems in trying to assess them. He was thankful when they ran out of time despite his awareness that while they had discussed things openly, they had made no progress whatever in developing a strategy for moving forward.

Vance's presentation of the proposals for maths was concise, logical and cynical. He used an overhead projector, but setting on and taking off the transparencies almost with distaste, as if he was handling slides of some sexually transmitted disease. At the heart of everything he said was his belief, reiterated in a variety of different ways, that maths was about numbers and the supreme goal should always be a high level of basic numeracy. In his eyes group work, projects, interactive learning were irrelevancies which only sought to distract from that basic principle. Vance's presentation turned into a statement of his personal creed and what was just as depressing were the heads nodding in agreement.

As Vance finished and gathered his materials together he

could feel the spirit of Reynolds seeping into the room. He glanced up at the postcard which was still pinned to the notice-board as if it was some holy object which couldn't be removed by mortal hands, and gradually he felt an urge to fight back, to take the situation by the throat and shake it. Crazy ideas raced through his mind, each more desperate than the other. He wanted to shout words at them, wanted to take their hands and swear sweetly and profusely. Wanted everyone to be shocked into something that would crack the rigid corsetry which hooped their souls and set them free for even one joyous sacred moment.

Watching them take their coffee break he felt isolated and ineffectual. Even Miss Fulton seemed slightly distant as if the day before had never happened and he wondered if perhaps she saw greater long-term security for herself in siding with Vance and Haslett. Maybe Liam Hennessy had got it right – keep your head down and let the shit fly overhead and stick somewhere else.

The morning dragged on and the sterility of much of the discussion was halted only by the approach of lunch. When the session ended there was a feeling of kids being let out from school, and as he gathered up his bits of paper he could hear some of them planning to eat out, but he was not invited. As he made his way back to his office he met George Crawford lumbering up the corridor, and a few minutes later he was sitting in his car being taken out for lunch. He sensed the purpose of his visit was neither spontaneous nor purely social. There was a flatness about his manner, an absence of his usual ebullience, but he kept whatever was in his mind until they reached a local hotel and had ordered their meal

'We have problems, John, problems with our friend the Reverend Houston.'

'The gaffe about the Girl Guides' display?'

'No, that's chicken feed compared to this one. He's gunning for you at the next governors' meeting and he won't be firing blanks. We need to get organised now.' He paused long enough to sip his drink. 'It's this Hennessy business and your EMU scheme – what a bloody stupid name!'

'Has he got some problem about it?'

'He's a problem all right and he's not the only one. But first let me get some facts right. Is it true that you've agreed to have a joint carol service at Christmas with Holy Cross?'

'Yes it is, I was going to get a formal go-ahead at the governors' meeting – I didn't think it was any big deal.'

'John, get the real world. Of course it's a big deal. For a start, since time immemorial the school's carol service has been in Houston's church with him doing it. A lot of the parents and local bigwigs come. So do you think he's going to be overjoyed when you tell him your news? And Vance, and maybe Muriel Haslett, have already poured poison into his ear.'

'It's nice to enjoy such loyal support.' They paused while the waiter brought their order.

'And where is this joint carol service going to be held?'

'I don't know George – it hasn't got to the stage of a formal arrangement or even a date.'

'In the chapel, the parochial hall? Is Father McWilliams going to be involved?'

'It all sounds a wee bit petty, George. It was just going to be a group of kids who've got to know each other singing a few carols. I can't see what the problem is.'

'The problem is you've been living in a nice middle class world too long and've forgotten what the real world's like. It's nothing to do with carols, it's nothing to do with kids. It's to do with Hennessy or more precisely, the Hennessy family and McWilliams.'

'I'm not with you.'

'Well then, let me spell it out. You've a girl in your school, in Vance's class, Lucy Ivors – a pretty thing with long blonde hair. Ring a bell? Three years ago her father Robert Ivors, a policeman, got up one morning, set off to work and at the end of the street a bomb stuck to the bottom of the car blew his legs off. He was dead when they got him out. The child watched the car burning from her bedroom window.'

'God, I'm sorry. I didn't know. No one ever told me. But what has this got to do with Hennessy?'

'Liam Hennessy's the oldest of five brothers – the word in the town was that it was Danny, the youngest brother, who did the job. He was never charged but the police believed he was the man. About a year ago the army shot him and another man in an operation out on the Middle Road. It's thought they were on their way to kill Martin Cash, a part-time policeman. The Hennessy family squealed about a shoot-to-kill policy and at the funeral McWilliams called for a public enquiry. Nobody ever mentioned Robbie Ivors.'

They both sat in silence staring at their plates. Neither of them had eaten very much.

'But Mrs Ivors never said anything, never objected to Lucy participating.'

'No and she's a remarkable woman – very strong and very in control. Not a drop of bitterness in her. I've spoken to her and she's happy for Lucy to take part in anything you organise. She's not the problem. It's others with less sense than she has. You know something, when Robbie was buried less than a week she got letters from some sick bastard, making fun of what happened. And if you don't believe that I've seen them.'

'What're we going to do?'

'Listen, John, I've nothing against Liam Hennessy. I run into him up at the races sometimes or in McDermott's when

128

he's open after hours. He's a decent enough soul and a bit of a character but as far as some people in this community are concerned all they know about him is he walked behind a coffin draped in a black beret and gloves.'

'It was his brother, George, what option did he have? Are you saying he approved of what his brother did?'

'No, I'm not, and I know he's spoken out against the people in the shadows who recruited his brother, but we're not talking about what I know. Most of our parents will be happy enough for their children to have a few outings with Holy Cross kids, some might even think it's a good idea but there's some, too, who don't want it and when they get themselves organised then we'll have trouble.'

'I know I've been away from town for a while but by and large people here have always got on pretty well – there haven't been that many incidents compared with other places. And do you not think that just maybe what we've started here might be good for the place?'

'Do me a favour. You think kids getting in buses and going to the zoo or the American Folk Museum is going to make any difference to anything? There's more chance of shit from a rocking horse.'

He could feel the tension rising between them and he needed George's support if he was to make anything of the job. 'Look – what about if we had a carol service somewhere neutral – the town square round the Christmas tree or some-where like that? No clergy at all. Would that help?'

'It'll not help the Reverend Houston and it doesn't solve the problem of Hennessy. I suppose it'd be something. Is there no chance of quietly ditching Holy Cross and taking up with someone else?'

'How can I, George? What am I supposed to say to Hennessy?'

'It'd make life a lot easier in the long run.'

'George, it's not even as if we're going to be coming together very often – two or three times a year maybe, that's all. And something that might appeal to you as a business man – there's a lot of money floating about for it. If we don't tap it, somebody else will.'

'Bugger the money – you'll end up bleeding for every penny of it.'

There was not time to discuss the matter further and on the drive back to school little was said. He did, however, agree to reconsider the whole thing. It wasn't even as if it was a great point of principle and he would have been embarrassed if he thought he was coming across in some naïvely idealistic way. It was just a good idea with a range of benefits for both schools. But the thought of dumping Hennessy was difficult to contemplate – what could he say that wouldn't leave him looking like some mean-minded lackey of small town prejudice?

A simple lunch together had given his staff a momentary sense of unity. It would have been a good thing but for the fact that he didn't feel included in it, and as he stood up to talk about assessment there was a drowsy, disinterested feeling which made his job even more difficult. His own interest had waned and he saw his best course as being to reach the finish as quickly as possible.

While explaining the legal requirements, making the safe assumption that some of them hadn't read the documentation sent out to schools, he found himself speaking the arid language of acronyms: at the end of each key stage there would be a CAI (common assessment instrument); teachers would have to decide the relevant TOE (tier of entry) for each pupil; to do this they would be helped by the evidence produced by EARS (external assessment resources). For a ludicrous second he felt he was making it up, as if he was telling them a fairy story where at any moment he might talk about a troll guarding a bridge, or mirrors which spoke, and he didn't doubt the expressions on their faces would have remained unchanged if he had. Nothing was registering, nothing permeated their tired indifference, and nothing he could say was stronger than their preoccupation with their plans for the coming holidays. He was in the way, the final lesson of the afternoon and he sensed their boredom transmitting into a sullen frustration as he rambled on, cutting corners in his discourse, becoming increasingly disjointed as he abandoned his planned structure. Mrs Haslett looked at her watch without disguise or subtlety. Anything now to be finished – he left out great chunks of his notes, obliterating record-keeping, records of achievement, formative and summative reporting. Then with a final few, rushed sentences he ground to a halt like a train at station bumpers and purely out of habit asked if there were any questions. The silence stretched taut and omnipotent, a thick sheet of ice frozen over the moment.

For a second it looked like Miss McCreavey was about to say something but she hesitated and then replaced the unspoken words with a vacant smile. Cutting short the embarrassment he thanked them and, before anyone could move, stood up and poured a glass of water.

In a few minutes only Mrs Craig remained, uncharacteristically hesitant, even nervous. He wondered if he was going to get an earbashing over the hole in her roof or some question he couldn't answer on assessment.

'John, I thought this would be as good a chance as any to let you know. I wanted to give you as much time as possible. I'm pregnant and I'll be applying shortly for maternity leave.'

He mumbled a congratulations with a forced smile and after giving him some dates she joined the others in the car park.

He listened to the sound of the starting engines and sat in silence for a few minutes then gathered up his things, only pausing long enough to pull Reynolds' postcard off the board and shred it into the waste paper bin.

*

It was still early when he drove over to the McQuarrie place. There seemed no other way of getting to speak to them – it was obvious they had no intention of coming to school. Though he had tried to find out about them he hadn't made much headway. McQuarrie had bought a small farm on Moss Road about ten years earlier and that made him a newcomer to the area. They had one other child, a boy of about seventeen who helped out on the farm and that was about all anyone had to report about them, except that they kept themselves to themselves. Because they didn't attend any of the local churches it eliminated one of the usual sources of information. Even his mother had been unable to provide anything more, except that she'd heard those who had cause to do business with him described him as dour and 'not given to wasting the time of day with you if he could avoid it'.

He thought that if he could call early enough he might be able to speak to them without causing too much disruption to their working day, but as he drove the short distance down country roads where a swathe of mist brimmed the fields he wondered how they would react. The car's wipers flicked away a clinging film of moisture as a dark clutch of crows glided across a whitened field before vanishing like spectres. The house number was painted crudely on a stone at the bottom of a long pot-holed lane which was rutted and bisected by a seam of grass. On either side a straggling barbed wire fence sagged where poles had worked themselves loose and sodden feathery heads of grass brushed the sides of the car.

As he reached the top of the lane he slowed down to get a look at the place before his arrival was noticed. It was an older, two-storey farmhouse, parts of it pebble-dashed and parts with what looked like recently rendered plaster – the new uncovered work squatting like scabs on the skin of the house. A porch extension had been built at some stage and its tiles were a different colour from the roof. In the windows of it hung blue, checked curtains and some spider plants in crocheted holders.

All around the house and sheds was a strewn junkyard of rusting farm machinery – tractors with their guts cannibalised, tyres piled on top of each other like a giant rubber toy, trailers and broken-backed ploughs. White-throated geese padded about and pecked at themselves in puddles, and smirched cats slinked through the fading wisps of mist which lingered round the base of the buildings. Out of an open-mouthed shed peered baled rows of black-polythened silage like rotting teeth and a straight line of milk churns stood stiffly reflecting the rising sun.

He parked his car beside the ancient Volvo estate which sat close to the porch door but as soon as he got out a shaggy mongrel set up a fierce barking and growled menacingly at him. He stood still, unable to gauge if it was bluff or for real, but knew that someone would soon appear to check the arrival of a stranger and decided caution was the best policy. In a few seconds a woman he assumed to be Mrs McQuarrie came out of the porch and without looking at him chased off the dog, flapping a faded towel. Only when it had reluctantly retreated and crawled under a tilting tractor did she turn to acknowledge him, apologising for the noise of the dog, and he sensed immediately that without them having met face-to-face before, she knew who he was.

She was a slight woman, perhaps in her late thirties but looking older, with fine brown hair pulled back tightly into a ponytail. Her thin, pale face bore no trace of make-up. She wore loose, shapeless jeans and a cheap sweat-shirt. He followed her into the kitchen which still had the uncleared breakfast things on the table and worktops, and as she offered him a cup of tea he almost stood in one of the metal dishes which was filled with slops for the dog – chunks of stale bread coated with milk and cornflakes. Pairs of muddied wellington boots stood on old newspapers beside a clothes horse buckling under the weight of drying clothes. She was flustered, embarrassed, and as she cleared the table kept apologising for the place. He tried hard to put her at her ease, to close whatever distance she felt existed between them, to use words which would put them on an equal standing.

'You wouldn't worry if you could see the kitchen I've just left. We still haven't got the house sorted out – it takes a brave while to get things ship-shape.'

She made him a cup of tea and neither of them mentioned the purpose of his visit as if his presence in her kitchen was an everyday occurrence.

'Do you like your new house Mr Cameron?'

'Aye it's fine but you get a lot of problems with an older house. We're having a bit of trouble with the septic tank at the moment.'

She rummaged in biscuit tins and set some down on a saucer. 'Hugh's down working in the back field – you'll be wanting to speak to him.'

'I'd like the chance to speak to you both but I don't want to take up too much of your time. If it's not convenient I'll call back another time.'

'I'll get Jacqueline to run over and get him.' She shouted into the hallway and before the final word of her call had faded her daughter was standing beside the clothes horse, twisting the sleeve of a jumper like a strand of hair. It was strange seeing her in her own environment and they glanced at each other with mutual curiosity.

'Hi, Jacqueline, you enjoying your holiday?'

She nodded her head without looking at him and under her woollen jumper he could see the outline of her Celtic cross. She was in her socks and a toe peeped out from a tiny hole.

'Are you going to do anything special?'

She looked up at her mother and fingered the outline of the cross.

'You know what it's like on a farm Mr Cameron – you don't get much chance to get away.'

'I know all about it, I grew up on a farm myself. Even when my father did take a break he worried about the place so much it wasn't worth going away.'

She smiled, and beckoning Jacqueline towards her and touching her hair gently, told her to go and fetch her father. She helped her put on the wellingtons, the two linking arms to form a balance, then searched down the boots to pull up her socks as far as they would go. As Jacqueline took her first steps the sheet of newspaper went with her, stuck to her sole, and everyone laughed. He stood up and with Mrs McQuarrie placed a foot on the newspaper on either side of the wellington until she was freed. As she ran off across the yard they smiled at each other, the simple act of help forming a fragile bond between them. After it she seemed more comfortable with him, less openly uneasy about his presence, but she still fussed round the table and unwashed dishes, using her activity as an excuse not to sit down. He felt a little more comfortable too, flicking through all the impressions he had carefully filed away since the moment of his arrival, anxious not to miss or misread anything. The woman was not an actress, too obviously uncalculating to carry off a deception. They made small talk and he asked her how the farm was going. From time to time as she answered she glanced discreetly through the kitchen window, anticipating the arrival of her husband, and he could sense her growing nervous again. As she became quieter he carried the burden of the conversation and he knew her concentration was not on what he was saying.

At the chugging sound of a tractor coming up the lane she stood up and confirmed it was her husband, then took a rag of a dish-cloth and wiped the draining board before turning to quickly lift away his unfinished cup of tea. He felt she was going to say something to him but couldn't find the words, and the only sound was water dripping into the sink and the welcoming bark of the dog.

'Mrs McQuarrie . . .'

She squeezed the dish-cloth into her hand.

'It'll be all right.'

She nodded her head and then went into the porch to open the outside door. He heard her whisper something and then McQuarrie came into the kitchen. He was dressed in mud-splashed blue overalls and when he pulled off his blue woollen cap he revealed a skim of thinning blond hair plastered flat to his head. A tall, broad-shouldered man with a face reddened by the seasons and outdoor work. He had blue eyes like Jacqueline and looked at the hand stretched out in greeting with open suspicion. He shook it quickly without excusing himself then turned his back to wash his hands in the sink, working up a lather from a thick block of green soap. She stood beside him ready with the towel and he took it without speaking, drying his hands in slow deliberate movements then handing it back to her.

'What can I do for you?' He stood at the edge of the table looking down at him, his hands plunged into the depths of side pockets.

'I'd like to talk to you about Jacqueline.'

Without turning McQuarrie called her from where she lurked in the porch and with the word 'upstairs' sent her scurrying into the hall.

He tried to be conciliatory, to create a positive atmosphere for what he had to say, and hoped McQuarrie would sit at the table. He made no reference to the earlier letter. 'I'll not take up your time – I know you're a busy man.'

McQuarrie pushed an indifferent hand through his hair and opened the top two buttons of his overalls. His wife hung back, close to the doorway, still holding the towel.

'As you're probably aware I'm concerned about Jacqueline's progress and don't feel that the school is able at present to give her the help she needs.' He paused while McQuarrie sat down on the chair opposite him, his hand sweeping bread crumbs to the floor. 'I'd like to have her assessed by the educational psychologist to get a clearer picture of what her strengths and weaknesses are and to get a recommendation about what would be best for her.'

'A psychologist,' repeated McQuarrie. 'People who are sick in the head need psychologists. My daughter's not sick in the head. She doesn't need a psychologist.'

'They're called psychologists but all they really do is chat to the child and give some tests in English and Maths. Find out their reading age – things like that.'

'And what'll tests show when she's done them except she didn't know any of the answers?'

'It would give us a more expert opinion on her needs and advise us what would be best for her.'

'You don't need any tests to know that Jacqueline's slow –

you hardly need to be an expert to know that and it's her parents who'll say what's best for her and not some stranger in a suit.'

There was a creak from the stairs and he knew she was sitting listening to her father's rising voice. His face had slowly flooded with colour and he sat stiff and straight-backed, his hands palm down on the table. Strong, squat hands, a rim of charcoal-coloured dirt under the broad nails.

'There are teachers trained to work with children like Jacqueline who really could help her make progress, fulfil some of the potential I know she has.'

'And where would these teachers be?'

'There are special schools and some schools have units which are able to do this sort of work.'

'It seems to me that teachers are paid to teach children, so are you saying that your teachers can't do that?'

'No I'm not saying that, but I'm saying we don't have the training, or more importantly the small numbers and facilities, to give Jacqueline the time and attention she needs.'

'Has Vance complained about her behaviour?'

'No, he hasn't, and it's not a question of behaviour. Jacqueline's a good girl. I know that.'

'She knows well enough that she's to behave properly when she goes out of this house. Isn't that right Lisa?'

His wife nodded her head.

'And tell me this Mr Cameron. Where would Jacqueline have to go for this help?'

'The Board would supply transport and take her to wherever there was a place.'

'Now you're supposed to be an expert, but you're telling me that it would be best for my daughter to take her away from the school she knows and all the people she knows in it and send her away somewhere she doesn't know anybody, and nobody knows her. Send her away every day to some school miles away and set her apart from all the other children here where she lives. Make a gypsy out of her. It doesn't sound very expert advice to my way of thinking.'

As he listened to his undisguised scorn he wanted to tell him about his child crouching at the base of the thorn hedge, curled like a mollusc on the rock, trailing her group at Nend-rum, but although he knew already that there was little he could say which would reach McQuarrie or alter his way of thinking he had to give it one final try. 'Sometimes children can be unkind . . .'

'We know that fine rightly,' he interrupted, 'and if you're really interested in Jacqueline's welfare there's something you can do for her, and that's make sure none of those wee skitters think they can get away with tormenting her. Because you can tell them from me that if I hear they're up to their old games I'll be up and tan their arses.' As he spoke his open palms clenched into hard knots of fists and one rose and fell heavily on the table making dishes and tea-stained spoons bounce like hail stones. 'Now Mr Cameron I've cattle waiting to be moved and work to be done. We don't all enjoy the holidays of teachers.'

Then pushing back his chair and pulling the woollen cap back on his head he strode out of the kitchen telling his wife he wouldn't be back until mid-afternoon. There was the sound of a tractor's reluctant engine and then it was gone.

He thought of trying to explain to her but knew it couldn't change things as she accompanied him silently to his car.

'Will you talk to him?'

'It'll do no good when he's his mind made up as sure as he has.'

'Will you try?'

She nodded her head with little conviction and then handed

him something. It was a jar of home-made jam, its little, stretched cellophane lid fastened with an elastic band. He thanked her and searched slowly in his pockets for his car keys. The curtain of an upstairs window moved slightly.

'Jacqueline's a bit of a tomboy isn't she?'

She nodded vaguely.

'She did very well on the outdoor pursuits day. Had a go at everything. Caused me a bit of a worry though when I saw her bruised arm. I thought she'd done it during one of the activities, so I was relieved when she told me she'd had a fall on the farm.' He found the key and unlocked the door.

'Said she'd had a tumble off the bales of silage.' She turned her head away as she spoke, her voice like the last faint wisps of mist.

'Aye you couldn't watch her. Those bales are very slippery when they're wet.'

He sat in the car watching her walk quietly back into the house before he turned on the engine. As he drove down the lane the dog ran alongside, barking and snapping at the wheels.

*

Emma was still in her dressing gown when he got home, sitting at the kitchen table drinking coffee. The signs weren't good. He set the jam on the table as if it was a peace offering. Her spirits had been sinking steadily over the previous few days but as a counterbalance they had planned to go away for the day, driving into the Mournes where they could do some hill-walking and she could sketch. On the way home they would stop and have an evening meal in an hotel. But now she moped about showing little energy or urgency to get the day started. From her posture and flat replies to his questions he sensed that in her eyes he had done something wrong. He had told

140

her a little about Jacqueline McQuarrie but not everything and she knew he had intended seeing her parents. It was obvious that the visit was something to do with her mood.

'Well are we going to get ready?' he asked.

'Ready for what?'

'Our day out.'

'I don't think you're very interested in going.'

'Of course I'm interested, why do you think I'm asking?'

'You're asking because you feel it's the right thing to do.'

He could feel his exasperation growing but, as always, resisted the temptation to say something forceful and plumped for the placatory. 'Emma, you were looking forward to it.'

'I was but I think it's a bit much that on your first day off you're away doing something about the school.'

'But you weren't even up when I left and I'm back now. It was something important – you know that.'

'John it's always important when school is concerned. And I know fine rightly that when we're out, about one tenth of your self will be with me and the rest of you will be thinking about school. Oh yes, you'll say all the right things, nod your head at the right times, but you're not really there. You're never really there.'

'You have to understand – I'm in a new job and there's a lot of things I have to keep on top of. It'll be easier when I'm in it a while longer and I've got things better organised.'

'Do you really believe that? Because I don't. It wasn't any different in your last job. Sometimes I don't think it'll ever be any different.'

She was angrier now than he'd seen her in a long time, the words bursting out of her and flowing over him, a hot lava flow scalding everything in its path. It was as if all the hurt and bitterness that had been stored so tightly were now finally breaking free. For a second he almost launched into a defensive listing of his virtues as a husband but stopped short because the first which came to his mind was the patience which he felt he displayed towards her at times like these. He tried his customary defence – lie back on the ropes and take the rage, shuffle a little, then deflect the flow in a different direction until gradually she wore herself out. But it seemed only to infuriate her more, provoking her to spew out words which would strike deeper, inflict some genuine hurt. As he listened, waiting for the rage to vent itself he tried to soak it up, to keep trying to calm her, hoping that it would all end with him holding her in his arms while she sobbed out the last dregs. But for the first time ever she was talking about their child, and in that moment they were suddenly shifted away from familiar ground.

'You think of yourself as the great carer – well did it ever occur to you that when I needed your support most it wasn't there for me? No matter what you say you only played at grief. I don't think you ever felt any pain inside. Holding my hand and saying everything would work out all right was about the limit of what you gave to me, and when you walked out of that hospital each night you went straight home to carry on with your cosy little world of school.'

He tried to deny what she was saying but couldn't explain about the suitcase: the words he used instead sounded cold and predictable even in his own ears. He had never seen her in such a state and it frightened him because he was no longer sure he could control or assuage her feelings.

'Tell me the truth John, did you really want to be a father?' She stared at him, the first tears starting.

'Of course Emma I wanted to be a father. I wanted the child as much as you did.'

'No, I don't think so. In fact I think the idea scared the hell out of you because while you go out of here and put on your performance, be Mr Wonderful to everybody else's child, you didn't know if you could carry it off with your own. And it would really scare you, wouldn't it, for a child, especially your own, to ever see you as less than Mr Wonderful?'

He tried to put his arm round her but she pushed the pathetic gesture away and rubbed her eyes with a shredded rag of tissue. He struggled to find some escape route for them both but only floundered further into the hail of her words.

'John Cameron, the children's friend, the great catcher in the rye. Why don't you admit it John, just once, that it's all phoney. From the day you found Maguire's boy you've been living off children, using them because they don't know any better, can't see what a fraud you are. You make yourself wonderful to them and live off their affection like some parasite. All their pathetic little adulation feeds your ego, makes you feel good about yourself and nothing else really matters to you. Just that alone, not me, and not the child we'll never have.' The tears were in full flow, smearing the pale wash of her face.

There was nothing he could do, nothing he could say. He opened the kitchen door and headed out across the fields.

*

The formal business of the governors' meeting was mostly bureaucratic in nature – the shortlisting of applications for a cleaning job, the wording of an advertisement for a temporary replacement for Mrs Craig. The Reverend Houston queried whether there was any need for the maternity leave to be advertised as one of his parishioners was looking for a teaching job and proceeded to give her a testimonial. Without being sure of her qualifications or exact experience he felt that in her involvement with church activities she had displayed enough

143

qualities of character to do a good job for the school. It was an argument that would have gathered momentum but for George intervening to say that while the good lady's application would certainly be considered, perhaps they should go ahead with the advertisement, purely 'to keep things above board'. Then after a long, rambling debate about whether the local youth club should be granted use of the school premises it was time to give his progress report on the term so far.

He tried to keep it as light as possible, realising that too strident a criticism of the school for which they had held a lengthy stewardship would only be counter-productive, and so he concentrated on the school's potential. He could see pleased faces as he expressed his gratitude for the opportunities the job had presented him with and he sensed the silent approval coming from George who was sitting beside him. He got a few laughs about his inability to get the hole in the roof fixed and someone made a vaguely dubious joke about Mrs Craig and waters breaking. As he sat down again he felt his chairman's large hand pat his back.

'I'd like to thank John for that very positive report and I'm sure gentlemen that you'll agree with me when I say that our school is in good hands. And I wonder if there isn't any other business if we haven't had enough for one night.' As he glanced deliberately at his watch Houston intervened.

'I'm sure, Mr Chairman, the governors would welcome the opportunity to ask Mr Cameron some questions.'

In an obviously pre-arranged manoeuvre Appleby, the local dentist, led the way.

'I was just wondering Mr Cameron, if you're sure that spending a full school day in outdoor pursuits can be justified at a time when preparations are still in hand for the transfer tests? I've nothing against them as such, but wonder if they wouldn't be better placed in the summer term after the test.'

'The centres are very heavily booked,' he said, 'often a full year in advance – and we took advantage of a cancellation. I can assure you that the children got a great deal out of it, probably almost as much as their headmaster.' He suddenly saw an image of Jacqueline jumping from the rock, her coat flapping open like wings.

The Reverend Houston leaned forward on the table and, giving his question a weighty air of formality, asked 'through the chair' which local primary school Mr Cameron had decided to work with in the EMU scheme. It was obviously a question to which the answer was already known but he received the information with a look of surprise, looking over his half-moon glasses with the air of a learned counsel who had just extracted some significant admission. 'And what prompted that particular choice?' he asked.

He pointed out the rather spontaneous and impromptu nature of the arrangement, stressing that it had no long-term commitment from either school, then he outlined the short-term financial benefits. 'And of course,' he said finally, 'before any formal arrangement is entered into with any school I will certainly consult the governors, but at this point the whole idea is still at an exploratory stage.'

He seemed to have momentarily out-flanked Houston and with George throwing in reminders of the lateness of the hour, the advantage was rapidly draining away from those governors who harboured reservations.

'Mr Cameron, through the chair, is there any truth that you're planning to have a joint carol service with Holy Cross?' The urgency of Houston's tone suggested he knew it was his final opportunity. 'This school has for many years held their carol service in our church where I may add that a great many of our parents are members and it would be a major disappointment if that tradition was to be broken.'

Before he had time to reply, Mr Gourley who had previously been silent throughout the meeting, launched into a rambling treatise about the fallacy of worshipping the Virgin Mary, the blasphemy of the mass and various theological criticisms of Catholicism. Everyone listened in embarrassment until eventually the chairman managed to intervene during a moment's pause and brought him to a halt, then offered the right of reply to Houston's question.

'I'm sorry Reverend Houston but you seem to have been misinformed. The carol service will take place as normal in St John's and we're grateful for your continued generous use of the church. I'm told it's one of the highlights of the school year and I look forward to it. We must get together and finalise a date and you can give me your thoughts on a programme – I'll be looking to you for guidance. We are, though, having a short carol service in the town square the final week of term – there will be a range of other schools there, including Holy Cross. I think the Council's organising it as part of their Christmas programme and afterwards we shall be distributing food parcels to the senior citizens. So if you have any elderly or deserving parishioners do pass on their names and addresses.'

As soon as he had finished speaking the chairman declared the meeting closed, and as the other governors gathered up their papers and made their exits, he was congratulated on his performance, George chuckling in satisfaction at Houston's failure. But he declined the offer of a drink, feeling only a sense of cheapness. As they left, Eric stood impatiently at the front door with his hand on the light switch, turning it off before they had stepped fully outside. As George said goodnight and lumbered off to his car he shouted after him.

'The right size for the job George.'

'Aye the right size John, that's sure enough.'

As he watched him drive off into the night, the red taillights seemed to mock him before they, too, vanished into the darkness.

*

She lay facing out of the bed, the stiff line of her back marking her inviolable space. He wanted to stretch out his hand, to speak to her, but something stopped him and he turned away. And in his dream the blackness wrapped itself round him, palpable, constricting, choking. Tiny flecks of light glinted like yellow stitches in a seam of coal. Now he is the one who is trapped. He shuffles across the coldness of the stone floor, his out-stretched hands feeling for some doorway into the light that must lie beyond. He calls out but the words vanish on his lips and as he stumbles forward his face feels webbed and veiled. He hears the sounds of people passing close to him, recognises their voices, then tries to call out to them but they pass on by. Flies buzz round his eyes and fasten on the smear of his hair. His hands are banging noiselessly against the heavy door. Then finally the darkness closes over him and he drifts into a broken and shallow sleep.

*

It was Laura Fulton's second day off. They would have to wait for another day before they would be able to get in a substitute teacher. He covered some of her classes and at other times the children were spread round other teachers ensuring disruption to everyone's day. To compound matters it rained heavily and was too wet to let the children out at break. They herded the older children into the hall and showed them a cartoon video he kept in his desk for emergencies. Water was dripping from Mrs Craig's roof at an enthusiastic rate and to amuse the children she had placed a little plastic duck in the bucket.

He had an informal interview with a Mrs Conway who had been suggested by Houston, but he wasn't impressed. She hadn't taught for several years, knew little about the new curriculum and talked more of her friendship with Haslett and Vance. As a short-term replacement she might have been reasonable but it worried him that if she got her foot in the door, and Miss Fulton decided she'd had enough, he could well find himself stuck with her. When she'd gone he spent some time phoning round other heads, asking if they could suggest someone, but he drew a blank. When he'd given up he phoned Laura Fulton to see how she was and when she'd be likely to return. It was her mother who answered and she proceeded to tell him how exhausted her daughter was, the number of hours she had put in every night on school work, about the collapse of her social life and how worried she and her husband were about her health. It sounded as if she blamed him for the situation. Their doctor had told her that she must take a complete break and wouldn't let her return until he gave his approval. She would be off at least the rest of the week and there was a vagueness about her answers in relation to a return which worried him, but he said little, apart from conveying his sympathy and his hopes for a full recovery. After completing the call he phoned Mrs Conway and asked her if she would start work right away and felt equal amounts of relief and regret when she agreed.

As he sat at his desk looking at Laura Fulton's timetable he saw that it was the period when she took Jacqueline for extra help in reading. He went down to Vance's room to collect her. The class were listening to some classical piece of music played on Vance's own CD-player which he sometimes brought to school. They sat up straight in their rows, arms

148

folded, each face staring blankly into space, as if listening to some foreign language whose meaning eluded them. He nodded apologetically to Vance and signalled to Jacqueline to come with him. As she stood up she tripped over the strap of a schoolbag and knocked her books to the floor. A snigger ran round the room but Vance silenced it with a look. She gathered up the books and replaced them on her desk, then, bringing her reader, passed up the aisle without raising her head.

He didn't want to intimidate her by using his office so he looked around for somewhere else. As they walked down the corridor he glanced out of a side window. It was starting to rain again. He saw Eric heading across the playground towards his house, a copy of the *Sun* held on his head like a flat cap. The wind billowed out his coat revealing a large pack of pink coloured toilet rolls. He took her into one of the cloakroom areas and found them two chairs but before he started to read he tried to get her to chat, asking if she liked Mr Vance's music. When she shook her head in reply he made her speak by asking who her favourite pop groups were. He'd never heard of them but pretended he had. They sounded like rap bands but he got no response when he asked about them further. He asked about her mother, said they'd enjoyed her jam and asked what her father and brother were doing on the farm, persisting until she made some kind of response. At first she spoke in single words or short phrases but he kept asking simple questions until gradually, as she relaxed, her replies became less closed and staccato. She spoke of helping her father on the farm, herding cattle along the road when they were moving fields, and he nodded his head with interest, watching her intently as she talked about her father.

She was wearing a grey sweat-shirt with a faded print of a Florida surf club and a grey pleated skirt with white ankle socks and cheap-looking trainers, the rim of their soles grimed with grass stains. On one of her knees was a crusted scab where she had fallen or banged her knee. He could see little pin-heads of grit in the penumbral skin around it but it was the type of mark that every other knee in the school wore – a kind of badge of growing up, of running too fast, of too reckless a jump. It almost reassured him, binding her to the other children. When she spoke her strangely pellucid eyes seemed to widen and dart about like small fish in a pool, as if enjoying the freedom but always wary of the watching world like some timid creature who comes to drink at a water-hole. Her skin was pale and unmarked, blending with the blondness of her hair which was cut in a shapeless style and suggested her mother had done the job. But despite the alert movement of her eyes there was something incomplete, almost unfinished about her features, like an image which hadn't fully focused. It made her seem younger than she was, vulnerable and unformed.

He thought, too, of the bruising on her arm, remembered her head falling like a stone on to her book, the stiffness of her arm the first time he touched her. Tried to weigh it against the other images – her mother touching her hair, pulling up her socks, the way she spoke about helping her father on the farm, McQuarrie's fist dropping on to the table. He had to be sure, even if it was only in his head. As she opened and turned the pages of her book, trying to find where she had left off, he stared at her and tried desperately to read what her face told him, but as he looked at her eyes there was only a limpid transparency which reflected nothing other than his desire to know.

She started to read, finger-pointing the words. 'Tom and Alison went on their bikes to Cherry Tree Farm.'

There was the now familiar faint scent of urine from her.

'It was a very sunny day and there were no clouds in the

150

sky.' She stuttered through the words, a pause between each one, her voice an unbroken monotone. 'When they arrived at the farmhouse their aunt Dorothy gave them a glass of lemonade and two of the buns she had just baked.'

She was identifying the words quite well, stumbling only a little over the unfamiliar syllables of the aunt's name, her mouth rehearsing the attempt. Occasionally he helped her but only when she had ground to a halt. He wondered how much she was assimilating but for the moment she moved on at the snail-pace which represented a struggle of concentration and determination. Like climbing a mountain, one tiny foothold at a time, resting on a safe little ledge where she recognised some familiar grouping of words, then staggering onwards, her finger probing like a blind man's stick. He wondered what would happen to her in life, wondered too what the world looked like through those translucent eyes (the blue the colour of some insect's delicate wing). Did she know her world was different from the children's she sat beside each day or was she happy within the parameters of her own world because she knew no different world existed? Tom and Alison on Cherry Tree Farm, helping their uncle set up stooks of hay, making a little wigwam where they had a picnic and fed crumbs to the birds. Cherry Tree Farm with white palisade fencing and yellow fields where there was no muck or shit or bits of tractors with their insides spilling out.

His eyes ran round the cloakroom – it had been one of the original classrooms. Mrs Preston had once given him a sixpence for his skill in reading, bringing him to the front of the class to show off. She had always picked him to read in carol services. One year he forgot to wait for the congregation to find the passage and he had finished the prophecy of Isaiah before anyone had time to find it.

It had grown dark outside. In the distance he could hear

music from Vance's room. He remembered the bored faces. He wondered if Jacqueline had made one of the fireworks in the foyer and as his thoughts turned to her, he was suddenly aware that she had stopped reading, the music from down the corridor had stopped. The only sound was the rain hitting the window. He looked up to see a pale face mouthing silent words, the lips forming wavering, voiceless vocables and he shivered as another memory washed over him. From some-where far off he heard his own child crying out to him, calling his name, and he stretched out his shaking hand and gently took the book from her and lightly stroked her cheek with the back of his fingers.

'It's all right, everything's going to be all right.'

She looked up at him with confusion but for the first time he was sure of what he had to do. He gave her back the book with its story of Cherry Tree Farm and watched as she walked back down the corridor to her class, her shoulder lightly brush-ing the wall.

In his office he rummaged in the filing cabinet, pulling out folders and forms until he found the one he was looking for. A pink double-sided page entitled, 'Request for Psychological Assessment'. He started to fill it in, her name, address, date of birth, parents' names. Nature of the problem, when he had discussed it with her parents, what steps the school had taken to try and help the situation. He signed his name and then looked at the only question which remained unanswered – the date when the parents had given him approval for assess-ment. He hesitated a second then filled in the date he had been to see the McQuarries, folded the form neatly and sealed it in an envelope.

*

On the way back from their visit to the Norman Castle at Greencastle he stopped the mini-bus at Annalong and the children tumbled out towards the shore. The tide was still out and beyond the wreath of grainy sand and the matted wrack of leathery seaweed, rocky peninsulas stretched like black fingers into the sea. They scampered about the beach, poking the seaweed gingerly with toes or bits of driftwood, nervous about what might suddenly emerge. Thomas Graham grabbed a wet-skinned branch and flailed it above his head like a charioteer, while others examined spent orange cartridge cases which had washed ashore, handling them delicately as if they might suddenly explode. The wind streamed everyone's hair and a couple of girls stood head to toe with it, their arms stretched out like scarecrows, their clothes rippling and flapping.

He watched them all from the blunted top of a wooden breakwater, fighting to hold his balance in the wind, as Norman Crosby discreetly pocketed shells he had picked up like a shop-lifter; Claire and Lisa swopped tiny bits of coloured glass, holding them in their cupped hands as if they were precious stones. The class was beginning to spread out too much and he tried to attract their attention and draw them closer by calling to them and waving his arms like a windmill. Putting two fingers in his mouth, he whistled shrilly, and as heads lifted along the beach he beckoned them. When they were gathered round in a ring of bleached faces, he made them all stand on the wooden breakwater and got them to copy him as he lifted one leg and stretched it into space. Spreading his arms out like wings, he told them to hold their balance like statues, then he jumped down and eliminated anyone who was moving.

After he had found a winner he raced them down to the water's edge and lined them up facing the sea. He showed them how to skim stones, how to pick smooth, flat ones, and when each of them took it in turn everyone shouted the skims in unison like a boxing referee counting out a fighter. They stood facing the swelling sea and skimmed their stones, cheering each skip and laughing when they sank without trace. Finding a washed-up plastic oil container he flung it in a whirling arc as far out to sea as he could and then everyone threw at it, only a rare hit making it buck. Above the wind he shouted all his oldest, most used sea jokes about seeing the sea plain, nervous wrecks which trembled on the sea bed, crabs arrested for pinching things.

They thought he was still joking when he suddenly pointed out the bobbing black head of a seal, but gradually they believed him and jumped up and down to try to see it in the trough between the waves. Someone else saw another head and then another, but they turned out to be a line of marker buoys and everyone laughed at the mistake. Then they clambered on to the rocks, peering into pools with an intensity of concentration that made him smile. Someone saw a crab and a group ringed the latticed and podded pool, squatting on their haunches, arms across shoulders to hold a linked balance. It had scurried under a stone and Martin Davison was rolling up his sleeve to dislodge it. He tried to scare him by warning about the size of the crab's lethal claws, and telling him about a film he had once seen about killer crabs which stripped the skin off their human victims, inch by inch, leaving the eyes to last. The boy hesitated and then in the face of his jeering, laughing classmates, plunged his arm into the water. A girl squealed and a couple of boys held on to his legs in case he would slide head first into the water. With a splash the rock turned over and under the covering cloud of sand and disturbed water the crab scuttled off to some safer refuge.

Gary Williams chased a squealing Dawn Clarke with a

crab's claw he had found and he had to persuade a couple of girls that it wouldn't be a good idea to go for a paddle. Soon it would be time to go. He watched them free-wheel about the shoreline, tattered and driven by the wind, oblivious to the time slipping by. Then, without being aware of her approach, Jacqueline was standing in front of him, her face pinched and blanched by the cold, her eyes pale flecks of blue. She held out her hand. He didn't understand. But then he saw the shell which she was giving to him. A white scallop shell ridged and perfect in itself. He took it carefully and thanked her. It seemed an important moment but as he searched for the right words she turned away, and before he could call her back two other girls came and sat beside him. He made them tell him a joke and then thought up impossible jobs for them to do – counting the waves, popping all the black pods of seaweed, sifting all the sand into a thimble. They thought up some for him – dive to the bottom of the sea and find a pearl, ride the waves, make a hundred skims.

A couple more joined the group and he told them about smugglers and the ghostly bell which could sometimes be heard ringing in the church graveyard. When he had finished they fired out questions, wanting all the unanswerable questions answered, but he promised to tell them more when they were back in school and then gave them the real task of gathering up everybody and heading back to the bus. He set them off but made them walk sideways like crabs holding their hands like nippers.

The sky was darkening now, the children standing on the rocks, silhouettes against the closing sky. Something in him wanted to stay, not to have to go back. The happiness of the moment began to fade as the thought of the imminent return spurred its own misery. He felt the salted sting of disappointment beat against his face. Nothing seemed to have worked out the way he had expected. He didn't know why. Emma, the new house, the school, all of them somehow tinged with a taint of failure. It was a feeling that was new to him but one which increasingly clung to him, no matter how he tried to shake it off. He summoned his talismans, gently turning the images over in his mind like the pages of a book – the sunshine through the slatted bars hitting the upturned faces, the lilting skipping song of the girls, even his moment of elevation to small town hero – but they seemed worn and frayed and couldn't drive away the mood fastening to him like lichen clinging to the surface of the rocks.

Since her outburst Emma had been quiet, moving about the house like some ghost and no words or actions on his part seemed strong enough to draw her back into her former self. She was polite, even conciliatory at times, but although neither of them spoke about the things that had been said, there was a consciousness that something had changed, perhaps for ever. Maybe she was right and he had been selfish with her, and if he had been able to love her more, would have known instinctively what to do to help her. Now he moved about her at a safe distance, handling her gently as if always driven by a consciousness of her fragility. She rarely painted, and before he stopped asking, she seemed unsure of how she spent each day, giving vague answers to all his questions. He wanted her to see her family doctor but even when she agreed, she put off making an appointment, finding one excuse after another. As he thought of himself more as a kind of nurse it absolved him of some of the responsibility of loving her in the way he had once done. There was a kind of relief in that, a feeling of respite from having to pretend to himself while outwardly there was no difference, nothing she would see or be hurt by. He never wanted to hurt her and so could never tell her about his dream, the dream that moved like a shadow through the night, seeking him out just at those very moments when he thought he had escaped it, had rooted out the spore.

School was wrong too. He had silently laughed at her belief that she could translate some glossy magazine image into a living reality, and yet he had constructed an image for himself of the school that he would miraculously transform, and now found himself increasingly unable to make it real. It had all felt so right, returning to where he began. He had felt so confident about it, so assured that he could achieve everything by just being himself, and now these few fleeting moments when he was able to be with the children were the only parts of his job which stirred any warmth or reward. He had given up the thing he loved and exchanged it for something which was inferior. It felt like he had betrayed all the children he had ever taught – the ones in the photographs in his office, the names in the roll books, the ones who were still to come. Betrayed the better parts of himself. He thought of Reynolds shuffling about his manicured lawn and brushing leaves into a polythene bag with liver-spotted hands. The right size for the job. He knew what it meant now as he felt his life encompassed by meanness, trapped in a small place in a small time, a future already marked out and harnessed.

The last of the children were getting into the bus. He fingered the delicate ridges of the shell and stored it safely in his pocket. The sky and darkness of the sea blurred and merged in the distance, the swelling waves surging towards the empty shore, the only light where they splashed and broke, white against the rocks.

*

By the time he had left the last child home it was quite late. He hoped he hadn't spoilt any plans Emma might have had for their evening meal, but when he parked the car he saw the house was in darkness. There was no light in her studio and the whole place was enveloped by a stillness. She hadn't told him of any plans to go out and as he had the car he couldn't think where she might have gone. There was no note to be found in any of the places they usually left them and the only sign of activity in the kitchen was a couple of unwashed coffee cups. He looked into rooms and switched on lights in an attempt to dispel the dankness which seemed to flow from the sullen corners and hallway.

The bathroom door was closed but there was no reply to his call and when he opened it he was aware immediately of the smell – gaseous, septic, angrier than it had been for a long time. As he stepped towards the windows to open them he saw the first floorboard, then another and another, ripped up with the claw hammer which rested on the floor, splinters of wood still trapped between its forks. Bent nails slithered across the floor as he kicked them without seeing them. There were half a dozen boards up exposing the criss-cross of beams, blotched and blackened copper pipes and a meshed twine of wiring. He knew she had done it, in some final desperation to discover the source of what had come to seem to her like a personal provocation, a malignant and spiteful incursor into their world.

He dropped to his knees and stared into the opened gullies, his eyes focussing on the steady ooze of water seeping from a hairline crack. It dripped down over a mess of rotting membrane and puddled into a stagnant slime. He stretched out his hand to touch it but pulled it back with a shiver, then pushed two of the boards over the stench. He closed the bathroom door and hurried into the bedroom. The crumpled quilt bore the imprint of her body. All her coats were still in the wardrobe and nothing seemed disturbed or out of place.

Taking the stairs two at a time he ran out of the house and across the yard into the outhouse she had turned into a studio. The fluorescent light flickered into an angry spasm of light which bounced off the white-painted walls. There was no sign of her, or her recent presence, but he looked around the room as if searching it for some clue as to her whereabouts. Picture frames and backing card were stacked on shelves amidst jars of murky, unchanged water. Some uncleaned brushes hardened on the table, their bristles stiff and splayed, blue paint squirming out of an open tube on to the board she used as a palette. There were a couple more coffee cups and some brown-ringed magazines, while on her easel was the current painting she was working on – a view of open countryside which he recognised as the view from the house. It was only half finished and didn't look as if she had worked on it for some time. When he went back out he left the light on, as if somehow that might reclaim the studio from its gloom.

Perhaps she had only gone for a walk, perhaps her parents had called and they would all arrive back at any moment. Maybe he should just put the kettle on and wait patiently for her return. Gradually he convinced himself that it was too soon to start to worry. Making himself a cup of tea he sat with it at the kitchen table, cupping the comfort of its warmth, and waited for it to cool. Then without having put it to his lips he left it sitting on the table and climbed the stairs again, this time stepping slowly and gently, listening all the time. Past the closed door of the bathroom and then another glance into the still empty bedroom, up the stairs to the attic. The door was partly open and he pushed it lightly and stared into the half-light.

She was sitting on the cane chair, the contents of the suit-case laid out neatly at her feet. In her hand was one of the cardigans his mother had knitted. She looked up at him as he stood in the doorway, frightened to step into the privacy of the moment, unsure of what to do or say. He saw no anger in her face or bitterness towards him, only the raw openness of her grief, like some scar tissue that would not heal. He felt a sudden burst of guilt, as if he had left her to deal with something which was greater than she could be expected to bear. Ignoring the possibility of rebuff he stepped towards her, calling her name, and like a child she stretched out her arms towards him, burying her head in his chest and crying without restraint, her whole body shaking as if convulsed. He stroked her hair, comforted her and held her tightly until she trembled to a pause. She borrowed his handkerchief and he squeezed on to the chair beside her, his arm still holding tight. She tried to say something but couldn't and he told her it was all right, that everything was going to be all right and they sat in silence for a long time.

Gradually he sensed her finding a control again but he didn't rush her, let her find her own time. And then, helping her from the chair, they both knelt on the floor and carefully folded and replaced all the objects in the case. Neither of them spoke but it felt as if they were facing what had happened together, perhaps for the first time, and then the case was closed, the metal clasps clicking in the silence. He led her down the stairs into the bedroom and they kicked off their shoes and slipped under the quilt. She clung to him as if she would drown in some fathomless sea if she were to let go.

'You would have liked a son John, wouldn't you?'

'Yes, I would have liked a son.'

'I always felt you wanted a girl.'

'A girl would be nice too. At least you wouldn't have to call her Phoebe.'

'You know something – Phoebe doesn't sound such a terrible name.'

'You always laughed at it before.'

'Well I'm changing my mind. John, do you think we'll ever have a child?'

'Yes, I do. We just have to be patient Emma – there's plenty of time for both of us. Look at Fiona Craig – she's four or five years older than you. Everything'll work out all right.'

For a second her body quivered in his arms and he thought she was going to cry again but she stifled it and went on talking. 'Sometimes I think it was my fault, that I must have done something wrong, that it was my body which let him down.'

'It wasn't your fault, it was nobody's fault.' He brushed her hair gently, caressed the nape of her neck.

'I wish it had been somebody's fault because then there would be somebody to blame, somebody to hate.'

'If we really believe it Emma, then we'll have another child, a boy or girl, it doesn't matter, but we'll have our own child and we'll both love it and then this pain won't hurt so much.'

'I don't think I'll ever forget it, sometimes I think the pain's never going to go away. It just seems as real as when it happened, sometimes worse. For a while I thought it was getting easier, just after we moved here, but then it all came back. I see something, hear something, and it all comes back.'

'You should have told me, maybe I could have been better for you.'

'You're always busy John, so wrapped up in school and the children that I find it hard to believe you've any space in your head for me. You shouldn't need me to tell you, if we were close you'd know without me having to spell it out.'

'Maybe it's time I started putting you first.'

'We're not close any more, not like we used to be. This thing should've brought us closer not driven us apart.'

'I know Emma, I know. I'm sorry, really sorry. Listen, why don't we go away this summer, rent somewhere in Donegal, spend three or four weeks doing nothing but pottering about on beaches and sitting in some tiny pub with a turf fire. You could do some painting – I was looking at your stuff in the studio and I think it's good. Some of the best you've done. We could go to one of those thatched cottages – you know the ones, quaint on the outside, all mod cons inside. What do you think?'

She nodded her head and he felt as though he was leading her away from the edge of the abyss, guiding her towards some safer path. He kept talking to her about the future, planting seeds of ideas and hoping he could slip something into her mind which she would hold on to, look forward to. She was curled into him and he told her again that everything was going to be all right in a repeated incantation of hope. The whispered words soothed her and then, exhausted, she started to slip towards sleep. As her eyes closed she told him she loved him, and as he cradled her gently he lied to her in the darkness.

*

He was vaguely conscious of the phone ringing in the kitchen. He hoped it would stop but it persisted, shrill and insistent, until it felt like it was ringing from the very inside of his head. He squinted at the alarm clock, saw it was 7.00 a.m. and couldn't think who it was could be calling so early on a Saturday morning. Emma slept on, oblivious to the ringing, still wearing her jeans and sweat-shirt from the night before. He slipped out of bed, stuck his feet in his slippers and hurried down the stairs. As he made his way to the phone he was sure that at any moment it would stop – it seemed to have been ringing for so long – but as he stretched out his hand to lift it, its sound didn't fade but seemed to grow louder in the sleeping silence of the house.

He had guessed at many voices waiting on the other end of the line but hadn't thought of Tom Quinn. At first he couldn't get a hold of what Quinn was telling him, couldn't translate the unbroken rush of his jumbled words into any coherent reality, but gradually their meaning lodged and registered in his fuddled, drowsy brain. As he started thinking clearly he asked Quinn a flow of questions but all he got in response was a re-hash of the original outpouring. Then he put the phone down and sat at the kitchen table, listened to the steady, somnolent breathing of the house. It seemed to arch over him like a giant bell-jar and he was suddenly aware of his own breathing, the loosening of his stomach.

He had an hour to get to the McQuarrie place. Too much time. He was sure that if he had tried to eat something he would be sick. He leaned back on the chair and looked at his hands. The fridge hummed and kicked itself into a louder whir. For some reason his mind flitted back to the early morning phone calls of his childhood. A couple of stray sheep that had squirmed their way out of a field, a loose cow wandering down country roads. Friendly calls from watchful neighbours, and his father would head off with the tractor and trailer, come back and resume his breakfast, muttering about having to spend the morning mending fences. Maybe it could be like that. Maybe it could be as simple once again.

He went to the sink and doused his face. The coldness of the water splashed him into a consciousness of the world outside. Thick frost sugared the windows of the car and behind it white-barked birch trees shredded themselves like paper. The silvered grass in the garden sat up in stiff tufts and the hedgerows glinted with a filigree of web. He filled the kettle and, unlocking the kitchen door, went and poured it over the windscreen. As the water dripped on to the bonnet he stood looking down into the blanched sweep of fields and shivered. A rabbit bolted from the bottom of the garden and vanished into the long grass of the bank. The gravel of the driveway felt compacted and clogged by the frost as he walked back to the house. He refilled the kettle and plugged it in. He should at least have something to take the chill out of his insides before he went out. Something to stop the churning.

It seemed to take a long time to boil and he sat again at the kitchen table wondering if there was anyone he should phone, but he guessed that all the calls that needed to be made had already been made. He was glad Quinn had phoned, wondered where he had heard. Going back upstairs he dressed quickly in his warmest clothing. As he closed the wardrobe door clumsily Emma wakened and looked at him in confusion. He sat on the edge of the bed and told her what had happened, tried to keep her calm, promised that it would be a false alarm and he would be back home soon, then he tucked the quilt round her and went back downstairs. He sipped his coffee quickly, trying to turn his head away from the smell and when he heard her footsteps upstairs swirled what was left in his cup into the sink and hurried out to the car.

He had to scrape the windscreen with the edge of a cassette case until he had cleared a viewing panel. The side and rear windows were still iced and as he started the engine it felt like he was sitting in a blind box. With a crack he unwound the two front side windows and then wound them up again, paring the surface of the ice. As he set off down the driveway he knew without looking that she was standing watching him, but he was no longer able to give any of his thoughts to her and concentrated on driving the car safely along the glittering roads, following the snakeskin patterns already printed. Soon the blower cleared the windscreen and as the heat started to seep into the car he was able to glance into the fields he passed. They sloped up from the road, a skim of white, static, lifeless, as if cemented into place, and nothing moved or broke the stillness of the morning.

There was a long line of vehicles parked in the verges leading to the McQuarrie place – cars, Land Rovers, a couple of tractors. A man stood at his opened boot, lifting out a pair of water boots and a waxed green coat. He parked at the end of the line and walked down the road to their lane. There was a policeman standing just inside the entrance but when he asked him the questions Quinn hadn't been able to answer, he politely pointed him towards the house. As he hurried along the muddied lane he could still hear the crackle of his police radio.

In the yard were maybe fifty men standing round its edges in tight little knots. Three or four dogs sniffed round the groups. The men were dressed in similar style – heavy farm coats and flat caps, boots, and nearly all carried sticks or poles. They looked like a group of beaters. One man wore waders. A police car was parked beside the Volvo and a constable stood on the doorstep of the porch controlling admission to the house. He looked round the groups, nodded to some of the faces he recognised. He heard someone say it had been announced on the local radio and then a figure broke away from one of the tight groups and came towards him. It was Quinn and he welcomed the opportunity to speak to someone and end his self-conscious isolation. He thanked him for the phone call then wondered if he should go and speak to someone inside the house, but there was no opportunity to do anything because the constable stood aside and a group filed into the yard. There was a police inspector and a policewoman followed by McQuarrie, his son, and another man he didn't recognise. Through one of the porch windows, behind the hanging spider plants, he caught the face of Mrs McQuarrie, holding herself back from the glass. He tried to catch her gaze but she seemed to pull herself back further from the clouded pane as if unwilling to be seen.

The inspector stopped in the middle of the yard and called the groups of men towards him. He told them little of the circumstances, only that she had gone missing the previous night, hadn't slept in the house and that he was concerned about her safety. His tone was neutral, undramatic, almost as if this was no more than some familiar routine. He thanked them for their response, told them the types of places to look, the areas which they were to concentrate on initially. It was when the first groups were starting to move out of the yard that McQuarrie saw him for the first time. He burst towards him, his face tightened into ugliness, the shouted curse bruising and tearing the stillness of the morning. He saw it coming – the broad band of wedding ring, the knots of knuckles swinging towards him – and although he twitched his head enough to avoid its full weight, it struck an arcing blow to the side of his face, burning and skinning his cheek. He felt the corner of his mouth split as if sliced by something sharp and then the taste of his blood.

'You bastard Cameron, you've no business being here.' He swung his fist again but his arms were clamped by restraining hands and Tom Quinn was pushing his way between them. Then others were ushering him away as McQuarrie struggled in his frustration to get at him, able only to spit obscenities. 'If it wasn't for you Cameron she'd still be here.' And then appealing to the police who were now the ones holding his arms. 'It was him that was trying to throw her out of his school because she wasn't bloody good enough for it. It were Cameron told her she'd have to go to another school, made

166

her sick with worry. You're a bastard Cameron.' They trundled him back to the house, his shouts still spewing across the yard.

He touched the broken skin but felt only the flame of his humiliation. He looked around him, saw their faces turn away from his. McQuarrie had stopped shouting but the words he had used still seemed to linger and fester over his senses like some spreading sore. The police inspector draped an arm round his shoulder and ushered him away with Quinn following protectively a few steps behind. They got into the back seat of a police car parked at the bottom of the lane.

'Are you all right?' he asked as he unbuttoned the top of his heavy coat.

'I'll live.' He dabbed the cut with his handkerchief and felt pathetic. He could taste the trickle of salted blood seeping across his tongue. He thought of the girl who had fallen and skinned her knees the first day of school, the red berries round the autumn display.

'McQuarrie's obviously upset at the moment as you can appreciate, but there was no call for that. If you want to press charges I'll act on it.'

'There's no need – it wouldn't help. Let's just find her.'

The inspector nodded, took off his cap and pushed a hand back through his flattened hair. 'So you're the headmaster then. What can you tell me about Jacqueline?'

'She's not academically bright – in fact she's very slow. She's got a reading and writing age well below her chronological age. That makes her a loner, an outsider – none of the other kids have much to do with her. I don't think she's been very happy . . . When did she go missing?'

'Some time between eight and ten last night. They thought she was in her room. When the mother called her for supper there was no reply. Have you any idea why she might have run away?'

He thought of the armlet of bruising coloured like a withering leaf, hesitated. Two men with sticks walked past, their dog
running ahead and sniffing in the verges. 'I don't know, maybe
something happened at home.'

'Parents say not. McQuarrie obviously blames you, says you
were trying to throw her out of the school.'

'I wasn't trying to throw her out of the school. She needs
special help, teachers who can give her the time and attention
she needs. We don't have the staffing and resources to give
her what she's entitled to.'

'Did you discuss this with the McQuarries?'

'Yes, I came to the farm, we talked about it.'

'And they weren't happy with what you suggested?'

'McQuarrie's not a man who listens well. He thinks his
child's happy. I couldn't make him understand. I could have
explained things to his wife but he obviously makes all the
decisions.'

'Do you have the authority to put her out of the school?'

'It's not a question of putting her out – I've explained that.
Decisions like this are usually taken in conjunction with the
parents. I suppose at the end of the day the Board could make
some decision but it would take a long time and they'd prefer
it to be a joint one.'

'The McQuarries had a phone call yesterday from an educational psychologist who says they gave permission to have
her tested. They say they didn't.'

The police radio punched voices into the car, call signs,
numbers, street names. A pale blink of sunlight filtered
through the windscreen. The car suddenly felt airless – he
felt an urge to open one of the windows. 'Maybe there was
some misunderstanding – I don't know. But should we not
be looking for Jacqueline, trying to find her before any more
time goes by?'

'People are looking for her right now. I just have a few more questions. Is she friendly with anyone in school at all, any house she might have stayed over at?'

'I don't think so, I really don't think so.' He thought of her crouched at the base of the hedge, curled like a mollusc on the slope of the rock.

'Might Mr Vance her teacher be able to tell us anything more which would be useful?'

He shook his head. The sun lit up the streaked dirt on the windscreen. Somewhere he could hear a dog barking. There was a frame of grime where the wipers couldn't reach. 'I don't think Mr Vance would be able to help but if you like I'll phone him. Are there no reports of anyone seeing her?'

'Nobody's seen anything. At this stage we can't rule out the possibility that she's been abducted.'

He looked into the man's face, saw the blue circles under his eyes, the tiny white scar high on his cheek and felt a spasm of sickness in his stomach. 'Abducted? That's not something you hear about in this part of the world. You don't really think . . .'

'It happens – not very often, thank God. But it can't be ruled out. Have any of your parents said anything about approaches to their children, seen strange cars hanging about?'

'Nobody's ever said anything.' He watched him put on his police cap then pull it down on his head and straighten it with the palms of both hands. They both got out of the car. 'Where do you want me to look?'

'I want you to go home Mr Cameron. The way McQuarrie feels at the moment it'd only be a distraction to have you involved. Go home and I'll ring if we hear anything.'

He wanted to argue but knew it was pointless. He would look on his own, keep away from McQuarrie. He started to walk back to his car, stopping when the inspector called after him.

'Mr Cameron, as often as not we find them sitting in front of some friend's TV with a bowl of cornflakes. This one's probably not any different.'

He raised his hand half-heartedly in an acknowledgement of the reassurance, got into the car and started the engine. He caught his reflection in the mirror, lightly fingered the raised weal of a bruise and the frayed corner of his lip. It made his face strange to him, unfamiliar, as if it was someone else who looked back at him. He drove slowly down the country roads, stopping from time to time at gateways into fields where he would get out and clamber on to the top rails, the metal bars cold against his skin, then stand up straight and slowly sweep the field. The strengthening sun had cleared the frost apart from those shadowed pockets where it could not reach and the earlier stillness had disappeared.

He passed others searching but he turned his face away and didn't look at them. His mind seemed incapable of focusing tightly on any single thought or plan and he drove instinctively, skipping from image to image like the wind flicking the pages of a discarded book. Only the word 'abducted' fixed itself in his consciousness, spawning a sadistic series of images with which to torture himself. The open door of a car, the appearance of an unfamiliar kindness, the offer of a friendship. But she was timid too, always pausing to sense the proximity of danger. Crouched down at the thorn hedge – only the blondness of her hair had made her visible and when he had looked again she had been gone.

He drove down roads he had already been down and all the time he felt as if there was something separating him from the reality of what was happening. It felt as if he was watching from a distance, rather than participating in it. Cocooned in the car it seemed he could reshape the events outside, if only he could bring his will to bear on them. If only he could stop the flicking, flitting images and take himself back to that moment before his hand lifted the phone, then the present might be rearranged in a different pattern. What was happening seemed to have originated inside him and had no life outside his own, but when he glanced in the mirror again there was the swollen ruck of skin to link him with the unravelling sickness. He pressed his palm firmly against it, tried to disperse the swelling, and thought of a lie to tell Emma.

If the child had left of her own will where could she run to? She had no knowledge of any outside world, no means of reaching it. Only these fields and hedged roads marked the meridians of her existence. And why had she left? Had something happened in that house, something that had to be hidden? McQuarrie's fist slamming into the kitchen table. The broad gold band of his wedding ring. The first time he had touched her, her arm stiff under his hand. Her head dropping like a stone on to the page. Maybe McQuarrie knew where she was, maybe his outburst had been only a calculated deception which masked some truth that could not be told. He saw again his wife's face fading slowly from the window, frightened to be seen by those gathered in the yard.

Why had he never told anyone about the wreath of bruising on her arm? Because he wasn't sure? Because he was frightened of being wrong? Because he was still trying to establish himself in this community and to be wrong would destroy the credibility he needed to succeed, replace that trust he sought with suspicion and doubt. But what if McQuarrie hadn't been acting and the child had really been frightened of losing the little the school had been able to give her? If that was true he would be able to help her understand, would still be able to see her. Perhaps there were arrangements that could be made so she wouldn't have to leave the school. None of it seemed important now in comparison to the need to find her.

He drove slowly up the driveway to his house. He wondered if there had been any phone calls for him, one simple call that would allow him to retrace his steps and start again. He tried to think of all the options that were open to her but it seemed a closed circle of an existence with no obvious point where she might break out. There was a light on in the outhouse – he remembered it had been on when he had been trying to de-ice the car. He remembered the hiss of the oil lamps in George Crawford's barn, the wavering, vaporous smoke of light. As children they had perched on the bales of hay and watched their parents dance in the crowded square of light. The moths. Drawn out of the darkness, fluttering round the trembling light, white wings like paper. Circling, homing, at last unable to resist the lure of the light. She would run to him – there was nowhere else. He jumped from the car without stopping to shut the door or remove the keys, pushed his way into the outhouse, but it was Emma's startled face he saw, and in her fright her hand knocked over the jar of water into which she was dipping her brush. Coloured water flowed through the broken glass, a little lake of blue lapping across the floor. She was staring at his face, asking questions he had no time to answer.

'Is she here? Did she come here?'

'Jacqueline?'

'Yes, is she here? Have you seen her?'

'No John, I haven't seen her. Your face . . .'

He sat down on the paint-spattered seat, fingered his face and told her the lie he had prepared, then answered all her questions as honestly as he could and stared at the blue splash of water and the jagged shards of glass. 'Emma, I have to find her. It's just possible that she's somewhere close by and that she'll try to come here.'

'What makes you think she'll come here?'

'Because she gave me a shell and . . .' He stopped himself, saw the confusion in her face. 'We have to look everywhere. There's no time to talk.'

He hurried outside, looking in the shed and other outhouse. He called her name, wheeling round himself in confused circles, shouting at the trees and hedges which bounded the garden. She followed, almost banging into him when he turned suddenly to veer in some new direction. His voice shot out across the surrounding fields, skimming the distance before disappearing. The silence was terrible to him and he shouted again and again as if hoping that it might scare away whatever it was that held her now. He turned to the house answering Emma's questions with an abrupt order to search. Every room, every hiding place. He bumped into furniture, richochetted into the hall and up the stairs, Emma trailing behind, trying to keep up. Their bedroom, the empty rooms, the bathroom where the pulled-up floorboards still littered the floor. She wasn't there. He slouched on to the floor with his back pushed against the bed and dabbed the corner of his mouth with the tips of his fingers. Emma stood in the doorway with blue paint on her hands. She was going to say something but he shook his head slowly from side to side and put a finger to his lips. Nothing passed between them and then he heard something – a rustle, a scrape of furniture, the press of a foot on a floorboard – and he was pushing past Emma who had registered nothing and was climbing the steep stairs to the attic. For a second his hand hesitated at the door and then he pushed it open, heard the whine of its warped frame.

A jumble of junk in cardboard boxes, empty tea-chests piled on top of each other like a child's building blocks, the cane chair, a closed suitcase. He had grown familiar with the sprawl and as he looked around him he knew that nothing had been moved, nothing touched.

'She's not here John.'

He sank into the chair and set it rocking. 'I know.'

He listened to her play the role that was normally his, as she came close and told him everything would work out all right, that the child would turn up safe and well, but her words left him untouched. He rocked harder on the chair, hoping that she would stop talking, give his mind time to think. Time to think about what was best, about what it was he had to do.

The hours dragged by, unremitting, irredeemably filled with the bitterest of imaginings. He wandered from room to room driven by a growing restlessness, eschewing all her attempts to reassure him. The phone rang only once – it was George Crawford asking if he'd heard anything but his voice sounded distant, almost cold. He spent some time phoning parents of pupils who were in her class but as he expected, none of their children had any ideas about where she might be. In return for no information he had to answer a series of questions as best he could and listen to uninformed conjecture and rumour. None of it was any help.

Sometimes he would go to the front of the house and look out across the fields and felt again the strange sense of distance which separated him from what was happening. He waited a long time before he pulled the curtains, pressing his face close to the coldness of the glass but saw nothing except his own reflection and the room in which he stood. They sat in the living room and pretended to watch the television, their efforts at conversation faltering and forced. He listened for the ring of the phone but it didn't come and although he heard it many times in his imagination, once even started towards it, there was nothing but the inane babble of the television. He went to the room he used as a study and sat at the desk, squaring the fan of papers into neat piles, straightening the pens and pencils. If only he could stretch out his hand to what was happening, pull it close to him, then he felt he might shape it into some order, guide it towards some safer end. But it felt veiled to him, always at a distance, swept along in its own flux.

He looked at the tea-chests, their heaped contents spilling over the sides. The titles on the faded covers of paperbacks and records seemed to meet his gaze with scorn, mocking the trust he had once placed in them. But there had to be something to trust, there always had to be something to trust, and if it wasn't any of the things which littered the chests, then what was it now, this thing he clutched to stop himself falling? Suddenly he started to pull at the clutter in one of the chests, shedding objects on to the floor until they formed a piled bonfire round his feet. A smell of must puffed up from the yellow-edged pages of sun-bleached books. He wanted to pull his head back but he burrowed on until he found it. A child's scrapbook, the corners of newsprint poking out from coarse grey pages. His name was printed crudely in block capitals on its front and there was a tiny blot in one corner where ink had leaked from his pen.

He placed it on the cleared desk, went and closed the study door, then hesitated a second before opening the pages, unsure, not of what he would see, but of what he would feel. He paused at the photograph of himself, the one taken at school which his mother had chided him for, and touched it lightly with his fingers. He turned the pages slowly, scanning the creased cuttings, their headlines playing in his head like half-remembered tunes. He sat for a long time and then gradually a calmness spread through him, stilling the flux and helping him understand what it was he had to do, what to believe.

He closed the scrapbook and held it tightly in his hands. There was something now at his core that he understood, this thing that he clutched to quell the rising fear. He saw everything clearly now, grasped it for the first time and pulled it close. Everything began to fall into shape, to assume an order where before had been only chaos. He suddenly felt a sense of his own goodness – of course he was capable of doing things that had no goodness in them, things that were mean and self-serving – but none of these could alter that awareness. It was rooted in the love he felt for the children he was given to care for – it didn't matter what Emma thought, there was something in that love which encompassed its own holiness, something which would always endure.

That moment in childhood, when he had stretched out his hand and touched another, was to be the given key to open everything that was now secret and shut away from the light of love. He had always believed in the past, preserved it pure and intact in his memory and now that very past would repeat itself, lead him to the same moment. The past and present had always to be linked, marked by the sure print of a pattern. If he didn't believe that then there was nothing to believe, for a man was chaff to be blown here and there by every wind that blew. Without a pattern he was only some straw-filled image of a man, lurching in a field, the random wind disfiguring his face and dispersing bits of him to the elements. His hand touched the bruise on his cheek, fingered the broken corner of his mouth and he knew that nothing could hurt him now.

Placing the scrapbook in the top drawer of the desk he left a scribbled note and opened the study door. He could hear voices on the television. Going to the kitchen he took a torch from one of the drawers then quietly went to the cloakroom and lifted his coat. Outside the coldness of the night stung his face and he pulled the coat tightly about himself. There was a pitted, smoking moon, fragile against the sharp-edged frieze of stars. He thought of the children's displays in the foyer of the school, spangles of light against the black sugar paper, and wondered again if anything there had been made by Jacqueline, if anything her hand had made nestled among the other children's creations. It was something he could ask her very soon.

He moved the car slowly down the driveway and out into the country roads. It didn't take him very long to reach the McQuarrie place. He parked in the same spot he had parked that morning, but instead of walking down the road to the lane he clambered over the fence into the field bordering the road and began a slow angled approach to the house. A tremulous, milky light filtered through the clouds and he used the torch to pick his way forward, stumbling occasionally when he encountered hollows and rises in the ground. As he got closer he used the torch less frequently and fixed his eyes on the yellow square of an upstairs window which quivered behind the swaying fingers of a black-boned tree. There was a ditch and more fences to be crossed. Once he had to push himself through a gap at the base of a hedgerow but he kept going, moving steadily closer.

He could see the outline of the house now, the curtained windows edged with yellow, the square of light that was the porch. Two outside lights arced into the yard and exposed the vague shapes of shed and outbuildings. He switched off the torch and dropped it into his pocket, then, standing at the edge of the yard in a pool of darkness, peered at the house, alert for any sound of the dog, but there was no sign of it or any other life. Gradually his eyes began to distinguish the disembodied contours of the junk which layered the yard like some moonscape. He half remembered, half saw some of the things he had seen on his two other visits; saw too in his memory the huddle of men who had stood round the edges waiting for their orders, the gold band on McQuarrie's fist as it swung towards him. Above him the moon looked like a reflection of itself on water. Skirting the edges of the yard and avoiding the arcs of light, he walked parallel to the house front, stopping when he was level with the porch. Suddenly from behind the hanging plants he saw a face coming forward to the window. It was Lisa McQuarrie and as she rubbed the condensation from the glass it looked like she was waving to him. She stood with her palms pressed above her head, her eyes scanning the darkness. He knew she couldn't see him and for a second thought of walking towards her, but instead held himself still and watched her.

Her breath steamed the glass and she wiped it clear. He wanted to speak to her. From watching her he knew that she didn't know where Jacqueline was. He remembered the way she had spoken to her daughter, touched her hair, and knew too that she couldn't hurt her. But there were other things that she might know, secrets that she might be able to tell if he could only reach her. He stepped towards the arc of light but as he did so she turned away and disappeared through the doorway that led to the kitchen. Only the prints of her hands clung to the glass. He hesitated, then stepped back into the darkness. An upstairs light went out, a moment later another was switched on.

Taking the torch from his pocket he made his way towards the metal shed, walking slowly and trying not to trip over the littered parts of machinery. The sliding door of the shed was half open and when he was inside he switched on the torch, letting the beam play over the stacked polythene bales of silage.

They shone in the light like black glass, the stretched surfaces taut like the skin of plums. From behind a row of metal milk churns slinked a cat, its eyes spots of amber. He directed the torch upwards into the metal beams of the roof where bits of machinery dangled from hooks. Something moved in the back of the shed. He spun the torch round on it and sparked a pair of eyes, the white of teeth, heard the deep growl rolling in the dog's throat. The torch lit up the stiffened back and the growl rattled like some engine as it edged towards him, low to the ground, its legs ready to thrust it forward in a charge. He took slow steps backwards staring the beam into its eyes, glancing around him for some weapon, but in the darkness there was nothing to be seen, and he didn't dare take his eyes from the animal for more than a second. He forced himself to keep his steps slow, his movements controlled, as he held his arm out stiffly like a stick, but as the dog hunched its back and tensed itself he half turned and in his panic stumbled over something. Falling backwards he heard the dog charging, the growl in its throat breaking into a barking that ripped the silence of the night, and he closed his eyes and swung the torch wildly, sending shadows skittering across the darkness. It was almost on him, so close he could smell its damp heat, its barking breaking close to his face, and then the swinging beam of light caught the rope which tethered it to some place back in the darkness.

As he stumbled to his feet the dog pulled against the rope and raised itself up on its back legs. Its unbroken barking seemed to crack the night open and, rushing to the shed entrance, he switched off the torch and ran across the arcs of light to slither into the shadows beyond. His breathing roared in his ears and there was a tightness in his chest. The bruise on the side of his face seemed suddenly alive, smarting with a new surge of pain that stung in the coldness of the night air. McQuarrie was in the porch – over his shoulder his wife's face and that of their son. He was bending over, putting on boots, his blond hair almost invisible in the yellow square of light. Taking a gulp of air he started to move away across the fields as quickly as he could, stooping and crouching as he went. As he ran he could hear McQuarrie's voice calling her name, over and over, and then two higher voices like echoes joined in the slowly fading wail.

He sat in the car, hunched over the wheel and tried to force his breathing into a calmer rhythm. In his head he could still hear the angry barking of the dog, McQuarrie's voice calling out, the two other echoing voices rising like a descant in the background. Over and over until they fused in a pulse of pain. He put his hands to his ears and tried to still his being. And as a calm slowly spread through him he began to think of secret places, of the secret places of childhood, his mind alert and listening, like the willow rod in the hands of the diviner passing over the hidden parts of his memory. He jerked upright. Maguire's place. He would find her in Maguire's place. He should have seen it. The pattern had its own power, its own inevitability, and he felt it now flooding over the years, carrying him towards what he should have always known.

He started the car and drove down the narrow lanes that carried him to that place. They seemed to funnel him towards it as if he had yielded control over his own volition. He drove slowly, trying to prepare himself, but in a matter of minutes had arrived at the laneway. It was too quick – he wasn't ready – and he drove by, went to the end of the road and then returned. He felt safe in the car, outside was the thick tide of night: cold, fathomless. He saw her holding the reading book, her pale face mouthing the words, heard himself telling her everything would be all right, and he parked the car and started up the laneway.

The leafless line of hedge jutted out at him, stark in the moonlight like coral, the slimy squelch of mud under his feet increasing his feeling of uncertainty. He shone the torch ahead, lighting up the greasy slope of the lane, and told himself that the slowness of his steps was caused by the uneven and sodden surface. He knew he would find her here, here in this place which stored its secrets like grass yellowing and rotting under a giant stone. As a boy he had watched it from the hidden folds of the tree, seen it always at a distance until that final day. He felt its hatred now, its implacable hatred for this person who had approached it like a thief and stolen what it had chosen to hide. He knew it would do him harm if it could.

He wondered what had brought her here and searched for a reason but knew it didn't matter. She had come, oblivious to the danger, and been trapped in some webbed world which held her fast and smothered all her cries for help. It was its way of hurting him after all these years, holding her now in some shuttered place where she curled, small and tight, and waited for him to come. He had told her everything would be all right, stretched out his hand towards her and she had believed him.

He was at the top of the lane now and in view of the house, the barn beyond. He had never approached it from this direction before, always having come across the fields. He went to the house first, the light of the torch making no reflection in the glassless windows, and shone it on the door that slouched in on itself like a drunken man. He called her name, heard it swallowed almost immediately by the silence and vanish echoless into some void. He called again and again but his words plummeted like stones into the well of night. He kicked at the door with the sole of his foot until it flopped free from its rusted hinge, then stepped into the tiny space that served as a hallway. Patterned shards of paper peeled from the wall. There was a cold dampness and the smell of piss.

He followed his light through the tiny rooms, his feet shuffling through the tinkling brightness of broken glass. On one wall was sprayed a scribbled babble of names and there was a blackened blotch in a corner where a fire had been lit. Into the front room, his splintered, shadowy reflection moving across the mirror. He called her name again, his voice ricochetting round the walls, growing louder and louder, until he spun away and hurried to the openness of the night. Outside he gulped the air greedily and flashed the torch across the yard. The sudden thwack of a sheet snapped by the wind. The axe buried in the yellow, rotten trunk of the tree. Almost tripping as he ran with it, his knee banging against the head. The shoes. The shoes bought in Dawson's with their clean white soles.

He turned towards the barn and with each step the whimpering grew louder. Louder and louder as he got closer to the darkness of the open doorway. But it wasn't like her voice, it wasn't like any human voice as it collapsed into a strangled, choking breathing. He hesitated at the entrance and called her name, called it again and again, urging her to come to him, to step out of the darkness, but at the sound of his voice the whimpering faded, replaced only by the wind rattling under the slate roof. He wanted the beam of the torch to be broader, its light brighter, as he played it into the shadows. She wasn't there – he tried to tell himself there was no need to go any further, but the need to be certain was greater than his fear and, dipping his head, he edged inside. He stayed close to the doorway and shone the light into the corners, and in his memory saw again the white frosted face, the tangle of smirched hair, the scab-covered spindle legs, and as he did so he felt the taste of his own sickness. He was conscious of something scurrying along the wall beyond his light but he pulled the beam away, not wanting to see it. He held the torch tightly, suddenly frightened that he might drop it and plunge himself into darkness. His hand was shaking and he supported it with his other one as he started to take careful steps backwards to the entrance.

He sat in the car, comforted by its familiar confines. Outside the night seemed to stretch edgeless and infinite. He felt some of his new-found conviction beginning to weaken. She hadn't been there when he had been so sure that was where he would find her, and once again he felt the fear of being part of something that was outside his control, of being carried along on something which he couldn't steer or stop. It left him feeling rootless, weightless, swept on by an uncharted current. He tried to reassert his will, to anchor himself again to the self-conviction which had seemed so strong a short time before. The full beam of the headlamps cut a swathe through the darkness of the high-hedged roads as he drove slowly, unsure of where he was going, the mechanical control of the car soothing and lulling him into a calmer train of thought.

He couldn't go home – he knew that – but there was nowhere left to look, nowhere he could even begin to imagine she might be. A car came round a corner and he fumbled clumsily to dip the headlights. He tried to think of his own childhood, of the options which he might have considered, but he couldn't pretend to himself that he had any understanding of how she felt or thought. And as he admitted that, his efforts to help her, to know her, seemed suddenly paltry, half-hearted. He had seen her as a symptom of what was wrong in Reynolds' school, and if he was truly honest, as a cause he could champion, a wrong he could publicly right. With a shiver he remembered what Emma had said about using children and he wondered again why he had said nothing about the wreath of bruising. Because he wasn't sure? Because he was frightened of being wrong and in the end more frightened of the consequences for himself than for the child? Each thought was sharpened by a sudden sense of shame. But it was still not too late. The credit he had accrued from that moment in the past, the years of caring for children – these, too, had to count for something.

On impulse he drove towards the town. He could see the link of orange lights somewhere in the distance. She was a child who lived in a world which was separate and unshared with anyone. Perhaps inside that world there was a place she felt safe, somewhere she would go to hide, to be invisible to the things that hurt her. He thought of the day he had discovered the copse overlooking Maguire's place, had climbed into the swaying canopy of flickering light and shade. To be invisible and safe – that was something she would clutch close like a secret. Small and safe, watching the world at a distance, breathing the stillness. Perhaps she had such a place and perhaps she was safe in her sanctuary, waiting for him to come.

He stopped the car some way from the school and walked to it in the shadows of the hedge. Across the road the windows of his caretaker's house were curtained and dead, but he hurried across the playground and unlocked the front door as quickly and quietly as he could using the torch. He couldn't risk switching on the lights. From outside the sodium lights lining the road speared orange shafts through windows. There was the familiar smell of school but heavily laced with disinfectant and polish. Only the absence of human noise made the moment strange, but the building seemed to creak and rustle with sounds that had no explanation. He could hear, too, the tick of the clock in the secretary's office, the stretch of distant

184

pipes. It suddenly seemed foreign to him, the corridors ahead lifeless and flat like some field of stubble.

His shoes squeaked on the tiled floor as he crossed the foyer and then he stepped on some dried-up leaves which had fallen from the display boards. He shone the torch up at them, saw the frame of brittle leaves and shrivelled berries. Some of the backing paper had loosened and sagged forward. Part of a firework had flapped free, revealing the cereal packet which formed its insides. It would soon be time to take it all down. He remembered the way the bare boards had looked and knew he would be faced with a constant battle to keep them covered with new work. Everything that represented a change from what the school had grown accustomed to would require the expenditure of time and energy. Everything would have to be pushed, nothing would roll forward of its own momentum. He had lost Laura Fulton and Fiona Craig and that had weakened his position, left him without a solid base on which to build. Some of his ideas would have to be put on hold, a few even abandoned. He fingered the bruise on his cheek and suddenly felt tired in the face of the struggle ahead of him.

His office brought no sense of comfort, the decoration provided by his personal memorabilia a spurious attempt to generate a sense of ownership. He shone the torch across the desk, lighting up the sliding pile of unopened mail. Some day soon he would cart it all out to the incinerator. He sat at his desk and listened to the strange pulse of sounds that came from far-off corners of the school. They made him shiver. He remembered the first morning he had sat there and listened to the noises outside as hundreds of children had scampered to their first class, and the feeling of loneliness that had brought. Trying to focus his mind again on the child he went to the filing cabinet and pulled out the manilla folder that bore her name, but the meagre lines of information created no image of her in his head nor produced any new ideas. He found it hard to visualise her face, to form any precise image, and he wished the folder contained a photograph. There was always something unformed about her, some pale absence of feature which made her blend with the background, bleached her indistinguishable from her surroundings. Only her eyes, only the blue of her eyes. He clutched at that memory, pulling it close to his consciousness, staring into it like the children had stared into the rock pool. It gave him a new sense of urgency, scattered the welling self-pity.

His steps in the corridor sounded loud and intrusive. He ran his hand lightly along the wall as he walked, his fingers feeling the pitted surface of the plaster. Past the closed doors of classrooms, past a frieze of the sea which Mrs Douglas's class had completed some weeks earlier. Blue paper waves, a yellow crust of sand, white chalk squiggles of birds, cardboard fish – all enclosed by a frame of real shells. He fanned the light across it and as he did so his hand caressed the contours of the shell he carried in his pocket. He remembered the sky and sea merging in the gloom, the silhouettes of the children perched on the rocks, the only light where the waves broke in jagged tatters of white.

He opened Vance's classroom with the master key. The room seemed smaller now, the geometric patterns on the back wall so close he felt he could reach out and touch them. The poster of Mozart, the neat piles of books. Vance's room. The children in silent rows listening to the music which cut them off from each other and from themselves. He could hear the music in his head as he stood in front of the empty desks. It flowed coldly into the corners and crevices and then contracted into the single solitary beat of the metronome which sat on Vance's desk. He wanted to shout, to smash it into silence.

And then he swore – a disconnected, meaningless orison of words, linked only by his need to stifle all other sounds.

He walked down the narrow row where her desk sat at the back of the room, her tongue peeping out of her mouth as she tried to keep inside the lines, the crayon clumsy and awkward in her hand. He stopped where he had stood that first history lesson and felt the stiffness of her body to his touch. He knelt down in the darkness at the edge of the desk and tried to look into her eyes, to look through them and catch some glimpse of what world lay beyond. He held on to the stanchions, the metal cold against his skin. The smell of urine, a blue biro streak like a vein on her cheek. But still she had no face, no precise expression or feature, like a map without contours or scale. Only her eyes were clear to him. He remembered her mother's face pressed against the glass of the porch, his own splintered reflection moving like a ghost across the mirror in Maguire's place. Tracing templates on to paper. Colouring them yellow for gold, printing her initials on the blankness of the page. The marks of her mother's hands hanging frozen in the glass like prints in the snow.

He sat on the wooden chair, his coat trailing the ground, and pointed the torch at the board. A frieze of perfectly formed lettering scripted across its top. Friday's date in the top corner. He moved the beam to the wooden units of shelving at the side of the board where text and exercise books were stacked. A neat pile of manilla folders. He moved the torch on then moved it back. A set of class folders. His knee clipped the top of the desk as he stood up and made his way towards them. Their names were printed in the top right corner and each one was devoid of decoration or graffiti. Only the occasional bruised grubbiness indicated that these were used by children. He flicked through them, spilling some on to the floor, until he found hers near the bottom of the pile. He carried it to

Vance's desk and sat down, holding it carefully as if it was his first link with the child.

Inside was a jumble of pages, some folded in on themselves, others creased and crumpled. He lifted each one out, smoothing the folds flat and set them in rows across the desk. Pages of large, loosely formed writing which slipped off the narrow blue lines and sloped away towards the edges of the page. Pages pulled from a colouring book and crudely shaded in. Drawings in thick waxy crayons. He tried to sort them into some chronological order but there seemed no connection between any of them. And nowhere could he see any sign of Vance ever having looked at anything or written any kind of response. He cursed him aloud, bursting the words through the tight clench of his teeth. He read the written pages carefully but mostly they consisted of paragraphs copied from some reading book, interspersed with exercises where she had to form the plural of words or change the tense of a verb. There was nothing personal, no expression of feelings or write-ups of events which had taken place. There was nothing which revealed anything about her life, no clues to what existed in her head. He started to replace them in the folder, shuffling them neatly like a pack of cards, then gathered up the pages of drawings. He was about to close the flap of the folder when he paused and held the torch close to the waxed crayon marks, then pulled it back to encompass all the pages. There was a similar pattern to them, similar colours. He propped them up against the book rack at the front of the desk and tried to make sense of them. Trees – they were drawings of trees, leaning in from the edges of the page towards each other. Trees forming an archway, the tops of their branches meeting. He could see it now – brown-barked trees shooting out meshed branches like a spider's web. What was it they overhung – a road, a river? He looked from one to the other. In

188

one the colour was green, in another black. It wasn't a river. And then he knew that what he was looking at were drawings of the old railway line.

He tried to fix the geography of the line in his head, to remember the direction it had taken them that Sunday morning when they had discovered Maguire's place. He took it slowly and calmly, working it out step by step, pushing along a straight line in his head which passed close to Maguire's place and then carried on towards the next town. He remembered the barbed wire fence which had blocked their path and then he knew that the line had to pass somewhere close to the boundary of the McQuarrie farm. He switched off the light and sat in the darkness. The wind rattled across the roof and vibrated loose glass in the windows. He had been wrong about Maguire's place, wrong about many things. In his hands he felt the softness of the paper drawings. Perhaps he was wrong now. His breath crystallised in the coldness and he pulled the coat tightly about him. Finding her would change everything, scatter every poisonous spore that had settled and festered on his life, make everything well again. He went to the window and peered out into the night. Even with the torch it would be impossible to move along the line in the darkness and he knew he would have to wait until dawn. But he knew, too, he couldn't go home, could never go home until he had the child in his arms. Locking the door behind him he made his way to the staffroom then switched on the one bar of the electric fire and pulled some of the chairs together. There was a blanket in one of the cupboards where first-aid equipment was stored and he lay down as best he could and pulled the blanket round him. He didn't try to sleep. If he slept he knew he would dream. Sometimes he slipped into a doze and then his head would jerk forward and he would wake again. Sometimes he imagined he heard children's voices in far-off corners of the school, the patter of their passing feet in the corridor. The talk he had given on the in-service day swam across his memory like eels, the words sliming and wriggling into constantly changing confusions. Once he glanced at the noticeboard to convince himself that Reynolds' postcard was no longer there, stuck like a royal seal on the ante-chamber of some sarcophagus.

The fire glowed red in the darkness but the thin element pushed little heat into the room and he curled his legs towards his chest. He got up to make himself a coffee but the jar had been locked away somewhere and there was only a bowl of brown-stained sugar and the sour, thickening remains of an old carton of milk. He lay down again and pushed the ends of the blanket under the cushions of the chairs. His mouth felt stale. Then he was aware again of his tiredness and he laid his head down and drifted into a broken, splintered sleep.

It was the cold which woke him and looking at his watch he saw that it was 6 a.m. In about another hour there would be enough light. He stood up and tried to stretch the stiffness out of his legs, then warmed his hands at the fire. He heated the kettle and washed his face, splashing the bleary redness from his eyes and patting the warmth of the water on to the bruise on his cheek. A tiny black crust had formed at the corner of his mouth and he touched it lightly with the tip of his finger. The coldness felt as if it came from his core and he shivered and placed his hands to the fire again. Some of the fluff from the blanket had balled itself on to his coat and he plucked it off as if pulling burrs from a dog. It would be warmer in the car. He switched off the fire and tidied the room, removing all trace of his presence. As he was about to close the door he looked at the blanket, remembered the sheet flapping and thwacking on the line, his father striding towards it, knowing what it was for. He folded it carefully, and opening his coat, pushed it inside his jumper.

In the foyer dampness had infiltrated further behind the displays, bubbling the pages like blistered paint. More leaves had fallen to the floor. Outside there was another frost, the steps leading from the school slippery under his feet. He sat in the car and turned on the engine and blower and waited. It seemed to take forever and he started to drive before the windscreen had fully cleared, the white cloud of the exhaust spurting upwards in his wake. Empty roads. Church bells still silent. He put the heater on full as the engine warmed and blew gusts of hot air into the car, then changed the focus of its direction at intervals. A yellow council lorry passed him in the opposite direction and he started as it clattered the side of the car with a hail of grit.

As he met country roads he drove more slowly, knowing that they would be untreated, and as he got closer to his destination he grew more nervous, his imagination generating a clicking freeze-frame of unwanted images. There was a grey half-light and with it funnelling spirals of white mist which snaked up from the earth like tendrils twining round the hedgerows and trees, smothering the edges of the world, absorbing and flattening all definition. It grimed itself like a cat against the windscreen and he flicked the wipers on to intermittent. Then into sudden pockets where the road was clear and untouched, while on either side of the road stretched fields thickened and coarsened by the heavy starch of frost.

He parked the car in a gateway to a field, paused a moment to check his bearings, then got out and headed for the broken haunches of a bridge which he knew must once have crossed the line. As always in such places there was a coil of beaten path which twisted down from the road into the track below, and he followed it, sometimes placing his hands on the spiked tufts of frozen grass to control his descent. Thick wedges of bush and trees tumbled down the slopes, long thin fingers of thorn cascading over the tops of lower trees and pushing through their branches. He started off in the direction he had decided would take him past the McQuarrie farm, pulling the cuffs of his coat over his hands like gloves and using them to prise back the springy whips of thorn. In places the track constricted into a single, narrow pathway and over his head pleached branches twisted through each other until their place of origin was uncertain.

In a little clearing he stopped for breath and felt the vaporous dampness of the morning press against his face and seep into his lungs. All around him were the vestiges of autumn – yellowing leprous leaves, large palmate leaves impregnated with black spots, browning, wilting ferns wearied by their own weight. He passed a plant rusted with strange red spots and in already bare trees squatted the exposed framework of birds' nests, like giant knots on the branches. Sometimes he stumbled as he walked, tripping over hidden stones or bits of rotting wood tangled and hidden in the grass. Ahead the path narrowed again and suddenly he felt afraid to push through the vaulted entrance. His breath streamed ahead of him. There was something he recognised, something he knew from some other time, some other place. It was the journey of his dreams – a long, unlit corridor of locked doors, a flight of bare stairs spiralling round a dark well, a laneway hemmed in by thorned hedges. He had heard the first whimpers when he was still in the car and as he pushed his way through the veil of branches they grew louder, insistent, pleading with him to come. Thorns plucked at his coat and water sprayed on to his face, but he hurried forward until he had forced his way into a clearer part of the track.

He paused again and pushed the droplets on to his tongue.

A rowan tree reared up its red berries in front of him and on either side the jagged needles of gorse were laced and linked by trembling web. He stumbled on, past a smear of withered hips, wrinkled like collapsed balloons, past the gorged seed-heads which brushed his coat. His pace had slowed now and on the hard, frozen parts of the track dead leaves rustled and whispered under his feet. He heard the child calling his name, calling out to him to come. He wanted to call in return but was frightened no words would break from his throat. He reached a damper part of the line where he walked over a blackened, rotting mulch of leaves, the sudden softness under his feet unsettling his balance. Each step he took seemed to stir some foul smell until it clung to his coat and he shook his head to be free of it. A child with his hair smirched with shit. A child with bowed, misshapen spindles for legs. He checked the blanket was still secure — he would need it soon, need it to wrap her in.

Emma was wrong. He would be the one to find her because he was the one who loved her more than anyone else. He was the one she was waiting for. He loved them all, more than Emma could ever know or be able to understand. Loved them because they were a living part of himself and because the strength of that love could save them from all the shit and sickness of the world. Hold them safe even for a little while until they were strong enough to make their own way. He would be the one to find her because he had been the one to stretch out his hand to touch the boy.

He stumbled on across a frozen stretch of water where the sharp spikes of reeds pushed through the ice. She was calling to him, over and over. He was getting closer all the time. The ice cracked with each of his steps, white rucks forking across its surface. The sound of the axe cracking against the door, the yellow wood splintering and splitting. His feet slipped from beneath him and as he stumbled he pushed his hand into the ice but he staggered again to surer ground where the track widened to its original width. Ahead, blocking the track, was the shell of a wrecked car, shining with frost and rust. For the first time he called her name, the words exploding out of him. There was a rustle in the undergrowth and two birds shot skyward at a sudden angle, and then silence again. And in the silence he heard the echo of his own voice and the strangled, choking breathing.

He had to force himself to go closer, each step a struggle of will. He fingered the shell like a talisman, prayed to the God he didn't believe in, summoned the upturned faces of the children washed by sunlight, the lilting chant of the skipping girls. Wheel-less, buckled, coated in rust, the car had been pushed down the bank from above, a broken swathe of scrub left in its wake. Jumping off the rock into the water below, her coat flapping open like wings. He had been frightened then too. Plunging below the surface of the water. The silhouette of the children on the rocks, the only light where the sea broke in white. It felt like he was walking into the waves, each one beating him back. His lungs were filling with water. He couldn't breathe. His foot caught something metal in the grass and he almost fell. He saw her through the glassless window of the rear door, curled in a tiny knot on the back seat. Curled asleep, her face pressed to the ripped upholstery, hands buried between her legs, her head swaddled by the piss-coloured foam pulled from the broad tears.

He whispered her name, frightened to waken her too suddenly, but she didn't hear him. He pulled the handle of the door and it cracked and rasped as it slowly opened. He looked at his hands – they were sprinkled with a sheen of rust. He called her again, louder this time, and gently touched the heel of her shoe, but all he could hear was the strangled, choking breathing which came from his throat. He knelt down beside her on the wet, rotting carpet and stretched out his hand. And as he did so he spoke to her, telling her again that everything would be all right, that nothing was going to hurt her ever again. He touched the side of her face with the tips of his fingers, then pulled them back as if burnt by the hoary skim of her skin. He lightly touched her hair, tried to smooth the stiff and tangled tails, brushed away the crystals which sat like spangles on her eyebrows. He tried to cradle her in his arms but couldn't pull the stiffness of her body into his. Like the first time he had touched her. He placed his knees on the front of the seat and rocked her gently. Over and over. His lost child, safely in his arms. Rocked and rocked. Then he laid her back down on the seat and covered her with the blanket.

THE LONG CORRIDOR stretched ahead to where shadows played in glass doors.

'Does he get many visitors Sister?'

'A few from time to time, not many.' She stopped to pick up a towel which was lying on the floor then turned to face him, folding it neatly as she spoke. 'Have you ever visited before Mr Cameron?'

'No, this is the first time.' He could feel her looking at him and it made him nervous, anxious to find the right words. 'I asked my parents a few times shortly after but they discouraged it. I suppose I stopped asking after a while. I wasn't much older than he was.'

She smoothed the towel flat with the palm of her hand and suddenly he felt like a little boy with a poor excuse. In desperation he played his best card.

'I was the boy who found him.' Immediately he felt foolish. He had told her something he had already told her on the phone. The words sounded pathetic – a child's attempt to claim some adult's approbation. As she set the towel on a radiator he felt the heat of his embarrassment flush his face and turned his head away.

'Come into my office for a few minutes Mr Cameron.' She gestured him wordlessly to a seat then sat behind her desk.

He hoped the redness had seeped out of his face and concentrated on regaining composure, some control of the situation. 'I suppose it must seem very strange to you, wanting to come here after all this time. I don't know whether what I said on the phone made any sense or not, but if you think it would be best that I didn't visit, then it's OK.'

For the first time he could see her relax a little. 'No, you can visit. Seeing a new face from time to time does him no harm. You understand we have to be careful. Sometimes we do discourage people – this is not a zoo, not a place to satisfy idle curiosity.'

He nodded his head to show his understanding of what she was trying to say. For a second he thought of attempting some further explanation of his motives but he knew he would have to lie to her and she was not a woman who looked as if she could be easily deceived. He would have to lie because he had no words to express the truth, was unsure of what the truth was any more. All he knew was the strength of the need which had brought him to this place. A need for what? To confess? To be given absolution? To receive a blessing? He didn't know. His fingers felt the damp spots on his jacket.

'You can see him for about twenty minutes. Much longer than that will probably prove too tiring for both of you. He has his own regular routines and too much deviation from them can be confusing and possibly distressing for him. He may, or may not, give you some response. It depends on the mood he's in – a bit like us all I suppose.' For the first time she allowed herself a brief half-smile. 'As you know he never developed the power of speech. At first they thought it would come but it was too late. He walks, not perfectly, but fast enough when he wants something. A few times when he's felt shut in or something's upset him he's taken off on us, but mostly, as far as it's possible to know these things, he seems reasonably contented with his life here. He doesn't give out a lot, keeps himself mostly to himself. Likes to watch television – I think that's what he's doing now in the day room. What he remembers or what goes on in his head would take someone more than me to say.'

She straightened some papers on her desk that were already straight and did not look up when she spoke again. 'I see a lot of sad things in my work and if you let them affect you, you wouldn't be very good at doing your job, but whenever I think about it it makes me shiver. It's hard to believe that such a thing can happen.' She looked up at him and he could see that she was embarrassed at revealing a personal aspect of herself.

'It was very terrible. Sometimes I dream about it,' he said quietly.

But she was deliberately looking at her watch, discouraging him from saying any more. She had closed herself off again and as she stood up he rose and followed her down the corridor to the day room. Once again she walked a few paces ahead of him and the only sounds were the clack of her scuffed white heels on the tiled floor and the crisp rustle of her uniform. He could see the doors ahead, the smear of fingers on the glass. Mrs McQuarrie's handprints on the porch window. Jacqueline's wet prints as she turned back to the changing room. The wreath of bruising. Always the wreath of bruising. Part of him wanted to turn and run, to run and never stop. But it was already too late. She held the door open for him.

It was a large room with a long window stretching the length of one side, affording a view of open countryside. The ebbing light of the afternoon filled the room with a shifting greyness, draining all the colour from it but no one had switched on the light. Tables and chairs sat in tight, inward-looking groups, comics and magazines stacked in neat piles, and the only colour in the room came from the television set which convulsed with cartoons.

'I'll leave you to make your own introductions. You can call in to my office on the way out and let me know how you got on.'

He felt startled by the abruptness of her departure which left them alone together in the room. He hesitated – all he could see from the doorway was his left hand on the arm of the high-backed chair, the thin white fingers splayed across the wooden armrest. On the coffee table in front was a remote control for the television. He stepped forward slowly, saw the side of his face for the first time. Smaller, younger than he had any right to be, a stubble of cropped hair flecked with thin slivers of pink skull, his eyes and cheek coloured only by the changing light from the television. He sat down on one of the chairs but the eyes stayed locked to the screen, the face a pale gleam in the gloom of the room. The light seemed to shape, then shade his face, moving across it like a shadow on water. A child who knew the world only through a fantail of light from an opening door, the chinks in the slats behind sacking. A child carried into the fierce, raw light of the world wrapped in a sheet.

He told him everything, holding nothing back, his voice strange to him as if it came from somewhere far outside himself. When he had finished the unblinking eyes still stared up at the screen as if he had heard nothing, nothing had registered. He grew more desperate.

'I was the one who found you. I was the one whose hand you touched, the boy you tried to say something to.' He stopped. The eyes had turned towards him, flicking over his face as if searching it for something forgotten, the mouth suddenly breaking into wordless speech. A hand was reaching out to him, reaching through the vistas of years, the pale glint of finger slowly crossing the space which separated them. He raised his own hand in response, then let it fall again, as the finger fell randomly on to the control and the eyes turned away to stare through the grainy striations of light at the picture trapped between stations, the rising pulse of static.

ALSO AVAILABLE BY DAVID PARK

THE POETS' WIVES

'Outstanding … Thoroughly enjoyable and much deeper even than the sum of its excellent parts'
IRISH TIMES

Three women, each destined to play the role of a poet's wife: Catherine Blake, the wife of William Blake – a poet, painter and engraver who struggles for recognition in a society that dismisses him as a madman; Nadezhda Mandelstam, wife of Russian poet Osip Mandelstam, whose work costs him his life under Stalin's terror; and the wife of a fictional contemporary Irish poet, who looks back on her marriage during the days after her husband's death as she seeks to fulfil his final wish. Set across continents and centuries these three women confront the contradictions between art and life, while struggling with infidelities that involve not only the flesh, but ultimately poetry itself.

'A marvellous triptych: lyrical, respectful of creativity but also sharply sceptical'
SUNDAY TIMES

'Park's tour-de-force … The depth of character and emotion […] are hallmarks of his work as a novelist of enormous sensitivity ****'
Dermot Bolger, **IRISH MAIL ON SUNDAY**